Tempting Turner

Published by Phaze Books
Also by Marie Rochelle

All the Fixin'

My Deepest Love: Zack

Caught

Loving True

Taken By Storm

A Taste of Love: Richard

Taken by Storm

Closer to You: Lee

Crossing the Railroad

Lucky Charms

Slow Seduction

PHAZE
Cincinnati, Ohio

www.Phaze.com

Tempting Turner

A novel of sensual romance by

MARIE ROCHELLE

Cincinnati, Ohio

A Phaze Production
Phaze Books
6470A Glenway Avenue, #109
Cincinnati, OH 45211-5222
Phaze is an imprint of Mundania Press, LLC.

To order additional copies of this book, contact:
books@phaze.com
www.Phaze.com

Cover art © 2009 Debi Lewis
Edited by Amanda Faith

eBook ISBN-13: 978-1-60659-149-9

First Edition – April, 2009
Printed in the United States of America

10 9 8 7 6 5 4 3 2 1

Dedication

Dave, thank you so much for being the reason why I wrote this book.

Marie

Chapter One

Sitting on his newly remolded deck of his Florida beach house, Dave Turner stared out at the calmness of the ocean. The warm night air-dried the sweat from his body after his nightly run. He had been home close to four months now, and he still couldn't get *her* out of his mind.

The last time he saw her was inside the hospital parking lot as she hurried past his black truck to her car. He had wanted so badly to jump out of his vehicle and stop her, but Charisma Miles wouldn't have stood for that.

He didn't understand why Charisma was putting up such a fight when it came to them. He knew that she felt the same intense attraction as him; however, she acted like he was a school boy with a crush. Hell, he left his boyhood in the past a long time ago. He was a grown man, and he wanted Charisma the only way a man craved a woman.

Sighing, Dave picked up his bottle of water and took a long satisfying drink. How in the hell was he going to fix this problem? He already had so many obstacles in his way. The timing was totally off. Plus, he didn't have any extra time to chase a woman who was pretending she didn't want him. His plate was full with raising his teenage sister and keeping her out of trouble. Did he want to add a partially snobby, yet drop dead gorgeous, woman to the mix?

Hell yes!

Dave knew that Charisma would fit quite nicely into his life, his bed, on top of table, and anywhere else he could get that sexy body of hers. But none of that would happen with him here in Florida and her hiding out in Los Angeles. He had picked up the phone numerous times to call her, only to hang it up after the second ring.

When he used to date the beach bunnies, he was usually the man with "the plan." But Charisma was pure class, from the top of head to her sexy toes. The first time he visited her office, it made him very uncomfortable. The men there had looked at him like he didn't belong. Sure, he still got the long lustful looks from the women, but he wanted more than that now.

Picking up his water, he took another lengthy drink while he thought about how tonight's college class was going to turn out. He signed up for a double major with computers and business administration, but the classes were kicking his ass. The computer part wasn't as hard because he got some early help from Jenisha Campbell. However, the business classes were way over his head, and most of the time he was too proud to raise his hand and ask questions since he was the oldest person in class.

The other students would stare at him like he was a big dumb muscular jock. He knew that he was intelligent and could accomplish any construction job that came his way, but Charisma needed more than that. She deserved a man who could pamper and spoil her. Shit, he wasn't a quitter. No matter how long it took, he was going to stick with the classes and graduate. When the time came again, he was going to be the man that won the body, heart, and soul of Charisma Miles.

"Hey, Dave. Why are you sitting out here staring out into space?" his sister asked, falling down into a patio chair next to him. "I thought you had a class tonight. Do you need me to help you with your homework? Make sure you answer all the questions right?" she teased.

Dave took his half-full water bottle and poured it over Brittney's head. He laughed as his sister jumped up out of the chair and brushed the water from her face. "Hey, you aren't funny!" she screamed. "This shirt cost eighty bucks."

"It better be your eighty bucks and not mine," he growled. "I've told you to stop writing checks on my account. You know I'm saving that money up so I can buy some stock into Campbell Construction and Design."

Brittney crossed her eyes at him before falling back down on the semi-damp patio chair. "You know that Hayward and Clinton like you enough to sell some stock to you at a lower price."

"Brittney, I'm not telling you again," he hissed. "Stop writing checks, or I might have to send you to that group home." Dave knew that Brittney wasn't in fear of him doing that to her.

"Yeah right, Like you would send me to the same place Mom and Dad pitched you at until you turned eighteen," Brittney sighed, placing a piece of grape gum in her mouth. "What's with you anyway? Ever since you came back home, you have been a bear to be around. Did you not get laid while you were in L.A.?"

Dave jumped out of his seat and glared down at his baby sister. "Why are you asking me something like that? Don't you have some kind of homework that needs to be done?"

Mumbling under her breath, Brittney dragged her five-foot seven-inch frame off the patio lounge. "God, you're really bad at changing the subject," she complained, popping her gum in his face. "I still think you're just pissed because you didn't get any while you were away," his sister hissed before she brushed past him.

"Don't worry about my love life," he snapped as Brittney closed the sliding glass door behind her. Massaging his shoulder, Dave walked down the steps at the side of his deck. The second the sand touched his feet, he felt all the stress leave his body.

This stretch of the beach was so peaceful this time of night. There weren't any people on it, and the wind mingled with the ocean air perfectly. He was only missing one thing, and he was going to get her no matter how long it took. The sound of his cell phone ringing drew him away from his Charisma fantasy, but it didn't matter. He could get back to it tonight in his bedroom. Taking the phone out of his shorts pocket, he answered it.

"Yeah, speak to me."

"I need you to come over here," the woman cried on the other end of the phone.

"Trish, stop crying. I'll be there," he said quickly, ending the phone call. Rushing over to his black Explorer parked in front of his house, Dave pulled out of the driveway, leaving a cloud of dust behind him.

Whatever was going on must be pretty bad for Trish to call him crying, he thought.

The last time Trish Mason called him for help was over two months ago. Back then, she wasn't looking for a helping hand when she called in the dead of night. He didn't even think that she still had his phone number after all this time. Trish was like no other woman he had ever met. She had an old soul about her that he admired and a way about her that drew attention.

Driving into the long spiral driveway of the three story red brick house, Dave got out of the car. Running up the steps, he only knocked on the door once, and it was jerked opened. A tall, slim brunette stood there tears pouring down her perfectly made face. "Thank you for coming. I need you so much," Trish whispered before she yanked him into the house and closed the door behind them.

* * * *

Several hours later, Dave strolled back through his front door, tired but happy. Trish had needed him tonight. It was a good thing that he didn't live that far from her, or he wouldn't be able to go there as quick as he did.

9

MARIE ROCHELLE

Running his fingers through his short haircut, he made his way up the stairs towards his bedroom. However, the loud screams coming from Brittney's bedroom made him race in that direction instead.

"Brittney, are you okay?" Dave yelled as he shouldered his way through her bedroom door. He stopped in his tracks at the sight of her holding a purple neon cell phone clutched to her chest. She was jumping up and down in the middle of the floor with a huge smile on her face.

"What in the hell in wrong with you?" he roared, his eyes taking a quick survey of the room not finding one thing out of place. "I heard you all the way downstairs."

"I won!" Brittney yelled, waving the phone in his direction.

"You won?" he said, confused with what latest scheme his baby sister was up to now.

Rolling her eyes like a typical teenager, Brittney hurled the phone on the bed and popped the grape gum that seemed rooted in her mouth. "The contest on sizzling 98.5," she grinned at him. "You're going to love it."

Don't let Brittney drag me into something I don't want to do, he begged. He hated when his sister did things like that. It always ended badly for him. He had six weeks of school left before he graduated with his computer/business administration degree. He didn't have any extra time to throw around.

"Why am I going to love it?" he questioned against his better judgment. *I'm setting myself for the other shoe to drop. I know I am.*

"You're constantly getting on me for wasting my time learning about the latest fashion, aren't you big brother?"

"You know I consider all of that a waste of time, so why are we talking about it again?"

Giving him a cheeky grin, Brittney rubbed her hands together, then spun around in a full circle and stopped.

10

"All that useless knowledge in my head just won us a two week trip to Jamaica!"

Dave's forehead knotted in a deep frown. "Jamaica! I can't take time off from school or work to watch over you in Jamaica. Hell, I have a hard enough time keeping up with you in the United States."

"See, that's the best part about it. I talked them into holding the trip for us until you graduated. The hotel needs to get a few more things ready. They'll call us when everything is finalized. Isn't this the coolest?"

"Yeah, it's the coolest," he murmured, turning for the door. Great. Now he would spend two weeks of his life pushing oversexed teenage island boys away from his flirtatious baby sister.

Chapter Two

Six weeks later

Charisma flung the pen down on her desk as she tried to keep from screaming at the top of her lungs. They couldn't do this to her, not after all the years she had put in at this damn job. How dare they give her an ultimatum about Lily Kane. She wasn't going to waste her time training her replacement. Did they think she was that stupid?

The partners knew she had been working her ass off for months doing any small job that came her way to prove to them that she could handle the bigger clients. But all Lily had to do was to twist those non-existent hips of hers, and the partners fell off their seats to help her. *Shit*, she wasn't going to fight dirty to landed the sports agent job. She had studied for months and finished her degree while teaching to land this job and a Cameron-Diaz-wannabe wasn't going to steal it.

"That tramp isn't going to win this battle over me," she hissed, storming over to her high-rise window. This plush office was hers, and she was going to fight until all her nails broke off to keep it. "Damn it! If I hadn't let myself get sidetrack by Dave, I wouldn't be here now."

A towering six foot six inches of male perfection flashed in her mind before she could stop it. Dave Turner had come into her life at the wrong time, and now she couldn't get him out of her thoughts. God, why did he have to be so fine? Jet-black hair cut close to his head enhanced his looks. That deep penetrating voice that he tried to seduce her with had kept her up for nights. Her water bill had jumped up a hundred dollars from all the cold showers she took after he left town.

Jenisha told her over and over she should call Dave and invite him to dinner. Never in her thirty-two years had she ever asked a man out on a date. Men flocked to her, not the other way around. However, if she was going to break her rule in her lifetime, it would be for "zero body fat, toned muscles that would make any body builder jealous" Dave Turner.

"You have to stop thinking about him," Charisma scolded herself. "He left town without even saying goodbye to you. How could you want a man like that?" *Because after that one kiss, you were horny for days.*

She shouldn't have let herself get sidetracked by a gorgeous face and even sexier body. Dave could fill out a pair of jeans like no one's business, and that caused her to be in the trouble she was in.

"Okay, you can fix this," she muttered to herself, trying to get her attention back on her job and away from Dave.

Lily wasn't the first woman to come along and try to steal her job. She just had to think of a way to make the partners understand she still had ice water running through her veins. Charisma Miles was still the hottest thing at this firm, and the sooner her rival knew it, the better.

"Charisma, can I speak to you for a moment?"

Charisma spun around and stared at her boss of three years, Easton Thurman. He was the only person who believed in her and gave her a chance to work for this company. She thought she could count on Easton to have her back, but he proved her wrong. What did he have to say to her now? Did he want to shove the knife deeper into her back? Just last year, she helped him land one of his top clients, and this is the thanks she got?

"Come in, Mr. Thurman." She moved back across the room and took a seat behind her desk. She didn't want to be standing up for any more bad news that might be brought her way.

"Charisma, I thought we were good enough friends by now to call each other by our first names," Easton sighed, closing her office door. He sauntered over to her desk and took a seat. "I know that you're upset about what happened in the meeting, but Lily has proven herself a lot in the past six months."

"Yeah, on her back," Charisma mumbled under her breath.

Easton leaned forward in his seat and stared at her. "Excuse me. What did you say?"

"I said, I bet she has," she lied, not wanting to get into an argument. She heard the rumors about Easton and Lily. She didn't have time to hear his lies.

"Charisma, don't be jealous," Easton chuckled. "You know that I offered you the same resources as Lily. She took me up on them, and you didn't. Now if you've having second thoughts, I'll be more than happy to give Miss Kane her walking papers."

Charisma swallowed down her first smart-ass response. She didn't want to get fired because she was working at her dream job, but she couldn't stomach the thought of Easton's hands anywhere on her body.

"My answer is still the same. I want to get ahead by using my brains and nothing else, Mr. Thurman."

"Fine….do as you wish, but I wanted to give you fair warning that Lily is going to have my full support. You're going to have to land some major players as clients for me not to give her your job."

Smirking, Charisma crossed her arms over her chest and gave Easton her best kiss-my-ass grins. "Well, I have always been a woman who loved a good challenge. Tell Miss Kane I hope that the best woman wins."

Laughing, Easton stood up and shook his head. "You still have that spunk I admire so much. It was one of the reasons I hired you."

She hated to ask, but she had to know. "What was the second reason?"

Walking to the door, Easton opened it before he answered her. "I wasn't going to miss the chance at looking at your perfect ass every day," he stated, going out the door before she could answer.

"God, I can't stand him now. How could I ever think he was one of the good guys?" Charisma fumed as she closed her eyes and rested her head against the back of her chair. She silently prayed that her day would be over before she knew it.

* * * *

Unlocking the door to her condominium, Charisma strolled inside kicking the door with the back of her heel. Placing her keys on the stand, she made it the six steps to her off-white couch before collapsing in the middle of it. *Damn!* She was tired and wanted to find a way to release some of this stress. She prayed her day would have gotten better after Easton left, but it didn't. Ten minutes later after her boss left, Lily sauntered into her office like it was already hers.

Lily didn't have a problem telling her how she was going to redecorate her office from the relaxing tropical theme to something more fun and sporty. It had taken sheer will power not to jump out of her chair and shove that bimbo onto her flat ass.

Women like Lily didn't move up the ladder by working hard and earning it. No, women like her seduced weak men like Easton to get what they wanted from the world. She had never been one of those types of females, and she hated other women that were.

She didn't know why she was complaining about Easton and his newest conquest. He had offered a helping hand several times, but she cut him off each and every day. God, sometimes the way his eyes followed her around the room freaked her out.

I need a vacation.

Sure. If she took a vacation now, Lily would have her job the second the plane left the landing strip. But it sure would feel good to get away for a month and forget about work and the other memory tucked away in the back of her mind; Dave "too sexy for his own good" Turner.

That man's sex appeal should be against the law or at least on the top ten most qualities one man couldn't possess. Dave had her body pressed back against Jenisha's couch months ago, and she still felt the imprint of his mouth on hers. She wasn't even going to think about the huge bulge that had also found its way between her thighs. Hmmm….she bet Dave was the kind of man that could make her body and mind relax of hours.

Don't go there.

She wasn't about to cross paths with Dave Turner again in her life. That was a once in the moment experience. He had been gone for months now and not called her once. It shouldn't be that hard for him to pick up a phone and ask a girl how she was doing. Why was she doing this to herself? Men chased her, not the other way around. But if she wanted to chase a man down and tie him to her bed, Dave would be on the top of her list.

All of that over six-foot frame would be undiscovered territory for her since she had never dated a man like him before. She didn't care that Dave was part Filipino and Greek. It had to do with the way he wanted to get inside her head and find out what made her tick.

In her other relationships, guys only wanted her on their arm because she was attractive, but Dave acted like he craved more than that. She couldn't get involved with a man like him. Short relationships always worked best for her. Her motto was 'no commitment required'.

Charisma stretched out on the couch and picked up the remote off the table. Dave Turner had taken up too much of her mind lately, and it needed to stop. Flicking on the television, she relaxed and waited for the commercials to finish running, hoping a good movie would come on next. Closing her eyes, she tried to get a few minutes rest because after experiencing Easton and Lily both in the same day, she deserved it.

"Hey, are you tired of working and need a break?" a male voice asked from the television penetrating Charisma's almost-relaxed mind.

"Are co-workers driving you up the wall, and you're at your rope end's? How about taking a relaxing, well-deserved two week vacation to one of the most beautiful places in the world?"

Opening her eyes, Charisma glanced at the well-muscular man on the television wearing a pair of shorts and no shirt making Dave pop right back into her mind. "Yeah, I would love to take a two week vacation to the most beautiful place in the world, but what's the catch?" she inquired under her breath. "There never something for nothing."

As a promo for the new *Chances Hotel and Spa* played behind the actor, he finished saying his rehearsed lines.

"For a limited time only, twenty lucky people will get an all expense-paid vacation to stay at this relaxing spa. So this might be your chance to find the man or woman of your dreams. Don't miss out on this opportunity. Your true mate only happens once in lifetime. Take a chance with the *Chances Hotel and Spa*."

The hot guy winked at the viewers and a one eight hundred number flashed across the screen. Against her better judgment, Charisma sat up on the couch and quickly jotted down the number. Placing the pencil down on the table, she looked at the piece of paper in her hand. Was she really going to call a number for a 'singles resort'? It wouldn't be like it wasn't the first time she had done the single's club thing, but the info commercial seemed a little corny to her.

"I can't do this by myself," Charisma exclaimed, reaching for the phone. If she got in, then it was meant to be. But if she didn't, the number would get thrown in the trashcan. Pushing her doubts to the side, she dialed the number before she chickened out.

"Congratulations, you're the twentieth caller," the voice recording answered on the other end of the phone. "Please hold while your call is being transferred. For being the twentieth caller, you get to bring along a friend at no charge. Once again, please stay on the line until one of our customer service representative can talk to you."

Lord, what have I gotten myself into? Charisma thought as a live person picked up on the other end.

Chapter Three

"Why are we staying upstairs so much? I want to go downstairs and enjoy the pool. I thought we came to Jamaica to have fun."

Dave turned away from the window and glanced at his sister standing by the hotel room door wearing a white bikini that he didn't approve of. "You aren't going downstairs dressed like that. You're showing way too much skin. Change that dental floss, and we can go downstairs."

"No," Brittney pouted. "I look good, and I'm going down to the beach instead of the pool. I want to get a tan."

"You don't need a tan, and you aren't leaving this room. Don't make me ground you while we're on vacation," he threatened, moving towards his baby sister. Brittney was testing his patience, and she knew it.

"How about I put on a cover up until I get down to the beach?" Brittney suggested, pulling a matching cover up out of her purse. "I swear I won't take it off until I get on the beach. Dave…please? It's our vacation, and I want to have some fun. You can go for a run on the beach and show off all those muscles. I know you'll draw some female attention."

He hated when Brittney played him like this, but he was running late for his afternoon jog. "Fine, but if I see one guy's hand where it shouldn't be, it will be over for him."

Running across the room, Brittney kissed him on the cheek. "Thanks, big brother. I promise I won't let any guy

19

feel me up," his sister agreed before she backed away from him and raced out the door.

"She's going back to our parent's house as soon as they get back from their cruise. I can't let her give me gray hairs," Dave said, reaching for the hotel card on the table. He looked around the room one last time to make sure he wasn't forgetting anything, and then left.

* * * *

"How did I let you talk me into this? You know I didn't have the time to take off for a vacation."

Charisma shook out her towel, laid it on the bench and sat down. She started pulling out items from her oversized straw purse looking for her sun block. "Because we have been friends since college, and I wanted you to come with me."

"You only asked me because Jenisha was busy with Clinton, their son, and the new baby," Keira Winters complained sitting down next to her on a hot pink blanket making her ebony skin shine under the hot Jamaican sun.

"That's a lie," Charisma gasped staring directly at her closest friend besides Jenisha. "You were the first person I thought of. I haven't kept in touch with the other girls from our sorority except you."

Pushing up her oversized sunglasses, Keira winked at her. "Got 'cha. I knew you would jump all over that. I know you needed this as much as I did. How are thing going at work anyway?" Keira asked, falling back on her towel. "Is Lily still trying to shove you out of your office?"

Rubbing sun block on her stomach and legs, Charisma rolled her eyes at the mention of her rival's name. "Yeah, that heifer is still breathing down my neck like a vampire thirsting for blood. Can't seem to shake her," she complained. "Easton is praising everything she does now and making sure I don't know about the weekly meetings until the last minute."

Flinging the bottle back into her red bag, Charisma ran her hands over her short haircut. "I can't take much more of the two of them."

"Don't you dare quit and give them what they want," Keira warned. "You've worked too hard to get that sports agent job. You fit that job perfectly. You love men, and you're around gorgeous men practically twenty-four seven."

Laughing, Charisma reached over and hit her friend on the arm. "Stop that. I decided to change careers because I wasn't living out my dream. I'm not going to let dumb and dumber run me away from my job."

"That's good to hear because if you were, I might have to knock some sense into that head of yours. Or meet you after work and the both of us have a little talk with Miss Lily Kane."

"See...that's why I loved hanging around you in college," Charisma exclaimed.

"So, it is my no-holds-barred personality," Keira grinned, wiggling her eyebrows.

"No, you didn't have a problem saying what was on your mind," she corrected, watching Keira grin at a couple of Tony Todd-wannabes passing by them.

"Damn, didn't they look good?" Keira sighed, sitting up on her towel pushing her sunglasses on her forehead.

"I don't know. I wasn't paying attention to them," Charisma answered.

"Umph. I know why, too."

"What are you talking about?" Charisma asked, leaning back on her elbows. "Now you know that I love looking at a ripped guy just like any other woman."

"However, you aren't interested in our fine brothers anymore after Dave Turner planted that kiss on you,"

Keira teased as she reached over and tugged Charisma's shades off her face.

"How do you even know about Dave and that kiss?" She snatched her glasses back and flung them in her bag. "I never mentioned him or the kiss to you."

"I'll never tell."

"You've been talking to Jenisha, haven't you? I knew I shouldn't have let the two of you go out to dinner two weeks ago."

"Honey, don't worry. I would forget about other men if a guy that sinful kissed me, too," Keira sighed, waving her hand in front of her face.

"You never laid eyes on Dave a day in your life. So, how do you know what he looks like?"

"Google."

Charisma gasped. "You found Dave on the internet? Is he a criminal or something?" She couldn't be interested in a guy that had been arrested. She liked a bad boy, but not that kind.

"Stop being so paranoid," Keira laughed, getting her bottle of water from her purse for Charisma before grabbing one for herself. "He used to enter body-building competitions about three years ago. Shit....that man has one killer body. Are you going to try him out?"

"You make it sound like I'm shopping for a new mattress," Charisma complained, opening her water and taking a sip. Keira always had a crazy way of looking at things, especially men.

"I couldn't think of a better thing to bounce up and down on than him, can you?" Keira shot back with a huge smile.

Chapter Four

The sun hitting his body made the run seem more intense than it actually was, but Dave didn't care. All he wanted to do was get his workout over and count the days until this trip was done. He was fine with Brittney winning the radio contest until he heard two guys talking on the elevator. Did his sister know that this hotel was also serving as a single resort? Hell, he would kill any of these grown men for even looking at his sister the wrong way.

No wonder so many of the women at the hotel kept slipping him their numbers, winking, or waving every time he passed them. He kind of felt bad for women who had to use this as a means to attract a man. Didn't they know just being themselves would have most men dying to meet them? Personally, he didn't think nothing was sexier than a woman who was smart and beautiful.

Ignoring the whistles coming from most of the females on the beach, Dave turned and ran into a more secluded area. He was about halfway down the strip when he spotted two very attractive women on beach towels laughing and talking. Both women were stunning in his opinion. However, one woman was the shade above obsidian, while the other was more cocoa with a shorter, spikier haircut. She reminded him of Charisma.

"Man. You have to get your mind off her. She doesn't want anything to do with you," Dave murmured to himself. Yet, he couldn't help but slow down as the females got up from their towels. Coming to a complete halt, the hairs on the back of his neck stood up as the

23

Charisma look-a-like spun around and their eyes connected.

Charisma, he mouthed before he took off in a dead run in her direction.

* * * *

"It can't be," Charisma exclaimed, stepping back so quickly that she ran into Keira.

"Hey, what is your problem?" Keira asked, standing beside her. "Girl, is that gorgeous specimen running towards us who I think it is?"

"Yeah, and we need to go." She tried to move around Keira, but her friend blocked her path.

"Sorry, it's too late for that. He's almost here, and I want to be introduced to the man that has you on the run."

"Keira Janice Winters, you better move out of my way," Charisma hissed, shoving her friend. "I can't let Dave get close to me. You don't know what it does to my mind."

"No time for a disappearing act. He's here," her friend laughed, moving out of her way.

"Charisma Miles, what a wonderful surprise seeing you here," Dave's voice broke in with a slight huskiness to it.

"You're a dead woman," Charisma whispered to Keira before she spun around and faced Dave.

She tried not to let her eyes wander over Dave's perfect physique, but she couldn't help herself. He was the most physically put together man she had ever seen, and it was such a shame she couldn't get into a relationship with the hunk in front of her.

"Hello, Dave. What are you doing here? I didn't think you would be the type to do the single's trip thing," she said, stepping back as far as Keira would let her move.

"I'm not. I came here with my sister. She won a radio contest for the same two week period the hotel was having their promotion." Dave quickly closed the gap between their bodies. "So, are you here for the single's promotion?"

"I'm a girl who likes to try new things," she grinned.

"From where I'm standing, you look like one hot woman. I don't see a girl's body standing in front of me," Dave praised as his eyes raked over her two-piece red floral bikini.

Charisma felt a pool of heat settle between her legs as Dave's tanned finger reached out and ran down the side of her arm. She wanted to shake off his light touch, but didn't. *What was it about him that made her forget all her dating rules?*

"Okay, before this turns into a pay-per-view movie on Showtime, how about you introduce me to your handsome friend?" Keira cut in, nudging her in the back with her finger.

She quickly shook off Dave's sexual trance and made introductions. "Charisma Miles, meet Dave Turner. He's friends with Jenisha and Clinton. Dave Turner, this nut beside me is my not-so-subtle friend, Keira Winters."

"Nice to meet you, Dave," Keira smiled. "Charisma has told me so much about you."

One of Dave's eyebrows shot up as he smiled down at her displaying perfect white teeth. "Oh? What has Charisma told you?"

"That you're one hell of a...."

"Keira, aren't you about to miss your massage back at the hotel?" Charisma snapped, trying to get her friend, and her even bigger mouth, to shut up.

"You're right. I have to go, but I hope we'll get the chance to talk again, Dave." Keira said, then grabbed her things and headed back in the direction of the hotel.

Charisma turned and stared at Keira until she was out of sight. Thank God she got Keira away before she blurted anything else.

"Your friend is very spunky, isn't she?" Dave breathed by her ear while his fingers stroked the small of her back.

"Keira won Miss Congeniality every year at the beauty pageant we had at college. She's a people person. I don't think she ever met a person she didn't like," she answered, moving away from Dave's magical fingers. "Well, I need to go, too. I have some phone calls to make back in my room."

"Why are you lying to me?"

"I'm not lying to you," she denied with a shake of her head. "I do need to call someone."

"Who?" Dave questioned.

"Easton."

"Is Easton your boyfriend?"

"NO!"

"Lover?" he growled between clenched teeth.

"NO!"

"Good, glad to hear that," Dave grinned, taking the towel she forgot all about from her hand. "Now, let's walk back to the hotel together. I want to know what time I should pick you up for our date tonight."

She barely stopped from stumbling over her own two feet. "I'm not going out on a date with you. How do you know that I don't already have plans with Keira or something?"

Taking her by the hand, Dave dragged her around a large rock at the far side of the beach away from the other people. Pressing her back against it, he braced his hands on either side of her body. "Charisma, we aren't going to play this game like we did in California. I know you want me."

Charisma opened her mouth to deny the claim, but Dave pressed a finger to her lips. "Baby, I want you, too, but on so many different levels. How about we take this time to get to know each other and see where it leads after that?"

Since she couldn't speak, Charisma nodded her head until Dave removed his finger. "I'd like that a lot, but I won't be able to spend all my time with you. I did come here with Keira as a girl's escape."

"Can I get you to spend your days with Keira and your nights with me? Keira's a cute woman. I'm sure she won't have a problem finding a male dinner companion," Dave suggested, running calloused hands down her sides. "I want to get you know you."

"You think Keira is cute?" Charisma asked jealously.

"Yeah…she's cute, but you're the one I want to spend hours making love to," Dave confessed as his wandering fingers slipped under her bikini bottoms.

"And from what I'm feeling, you want the same thing," he chuckled, slipping two thick fingers inside of her.

"No. You can't do that here," Charisma hissed, touching Dave's forearm. She swallowed hard to keep from moaning. *How long had it been since a man touched her like this*?

Bending his head, Dave licked the side of her neck, and then whispered in her ear. "Are you a virgin?"

"How is that any of your business?" she asked, tugging at his arm. Dave wasn't about to judge her because she wasn't a virgin. She truly doubted that he was one, either.

"If you answer my question, you'll find out why I asked it," Dave whispered as he continued to move his fingers lightly in and out of her traitorous body.

"That ship sailed years ago," she sighed, dropping her hand while getting lost in the moment of Dave and what he was doing to her. Charisma's body was at a low hum as the sensation of Dave's fingers learned the tempo she craved.

"Excellent. Those are the words that I wanted to hear," Dave exclaimed a spilt second before his thick fingers thrust into her wetness to the hilt.

Her orgasm hit her so fast and hard that Dave almost didn't silence her screams in time with his mouth. But the thought of being silent didn't enter her mind as wave after wave of ecstasy shattered her body, mind, and soul.

* * * *

Dave wanted so badly to move the necessary articles of clothing out of the way and be enveloped by Charisma's heat, but he couldn't. So he kissed her instead; however, that wasn't giving him what he wanted or needed.

Taking his fingers out of her quivering body, he moved them to cup Charisma's perfect butt and held her to him while her orgasm rocket through her making his cock harder than it had ever been. He knew this special moment wouldn't last, so he enjoyed it while he could. Removing his lips from hers, he trailed them down the side of her neck, kissing the pulse that pounded there. Only a few seconds passed before he felt Charisma's hands shove at his chest, and she was twisting her body trying to get away from him.

"What in the hell are we doing out in the open like this? Anyone could have passed by and seen us!" Charisma hissed, fixing her bathing suit and glancing around the deserted stretch of beach.

"Is that an offer to join you upstairs in your room?" he asked, running his fingers between her breasts. "I would love to see this beautiful body of yours naked while I make love to you."

Charisma shot him a look and knocked his fingers off her body. "Don't go there with me. You caught me at a weak moment, but it won't happen again." Turning away from him, she picked up her bag off the sand and moved away from him.

His hand shot out and wrapped around Charisma's waist jerking her silky body back to his aroused one. "Did I catch you at a bad time when you let me kiss you at Jenisha's house all those months ago?" he inquired, sliding his hands up to cup her breast. "I seem to remember that you let me kiss the hell out of you then, too, and enjoyed it." Dave quickly undid the front of Charisma's bikini and his fingers fondled her nipples loving how they grew even harder.

"Oh....you have to stop," Charisma moaned as her head fell back against his shoulder. "We can't do this."

"Why can't we?" Dave whispered as he eased his other hand into her bikini bottoms and smiled when her juices soaked his fingers. "You know that I find you attractive and if this in any indication," he whispered stroking Charisma's damp curls, "you find me a little attractive, too. So why don't we act on those feelings?"

"Dave...you have to..." Charisma started to answer, but went still when the sound of voices approaching started to come toward them.

"Man, I know I saw the football fly over this away," a male voice yelled as it got closer to them.

Dave cursed under his breath as Charisma practically flew out of his arms and fixed her clothes. He was making such progress with her, and now all of it was probably ruined. She wasn't about to let him within twenty feet of her unless he found a way to make her understand they were meant to be together.

He watched while Charisma snatched up her bag and pressed it against her chest. "You stay away from me. I mean it, Dave Turner. Don't come near me while you're here," Charisma demanded then spun away from him and hurried across the sand back in the direction of the hotel.

"Charisma, wait," Dave screamed after her retreating figure, but he knew that she wouldn't. He started after her, but stopped when a voice yelled behind him.

"Hey man, have you seen our football? I'm sure it flew over this way."

Swallowing down nasty comment, Dave spun around and glared at the blond guy standing a few feet behind him. "No, I haven't seen your football. Are you sure it came over this away?"

"I was positive that it did, but thanks away," the guy answered, then spun around and went back the way he came.

Dave pivoted hoping to see Charisma, but the beach was empty: however, he wasn't about to give up. After that explosive moment they just shared, it proved to him that she was his. Now all he had to do was make her see it, too.

"Charisma, run all that you want, but in the end you will be mine," he promised himself, then went back to his run. *I don't think this trip is such a bad idea now*, Dave thought as his feet ran across the sandy beach.

Chapter Five

"Young lady, where have you been all this time, and don't you dare lie to me."

Spinning away from the closed door, Charisma's eyes flew over to the adjoining hotel room door and glared at Keira standing there wearing a thick fluffy robe. "You scared the hell out of me. Don't do that again," she snapped, coming the rest of the way into the room.

"Hey, I wasn't the one sneaking back into my room like I had missed curfew," Keira teased, arching one eyebrow. "Have you been doing something that you shouldn't with that hunky Dave Turner?"

Why would Keira ask her that? Did she really look guilty of something? Running her hands over her short hair, Charisma shook her head and her friend and lied. "No, I haven't been doing anything I shouldn't. I stayed and talked to Dave for a few minutes, then left him on the beach." She threw her bag on the futon and made her way over to her bedroom. "Why would you ask me something like that?"

"Oh, I don't know. Maybe it has to do with the fact that your left breast is about to pop out of your top," Keira commented as she followed her into her room. "I know it just didn't fall out on its own, now did it?"

Damn it!

She shoved her breast back into the top and adjusted the bottom. Charisma couldn't tell Keira about what happened back on the beach. It was way too embarrassing

31

that she made herself that available to Dave. She was going to make sure it didn't happen again.

"I don't know what happened. You know how it can be when it comes to these tops. One minute everything is in place, and the next breath a Janet Jackson malfunction happens."

"Hon…I hope you know that isn't going to fly with me," Keira scolded, falling down on the middle of the bed. The bed bounced as her weight hit directly in the middle of the mattress. "Dave is one sexy looking man. I know you didn't get away without him at least kissing you."

Why did she think Jenisha was the bad one when it came to digging out the truth? Hell, Keira was twenty times worst. "Maybe he did kiss me," Charisma finally admitted as she made her way over to her closet. "But I'm not going to tell you anything else, because I don't want to."

"You don't have to say another word," Keira giggled, getting up from the bed. "I can tell more happened from just looking at you."

"What are you talking about?" Charisma asked as she pulled a dress from the closet to wear to dinner tonight. What was different about her? Had Dave done something that she didn't know about? He had the ability to distract her all the time. She had to stay on her game better, or he'll end up breaking her down.

"Girl…you have this glow about you that you didn't have when I left you on the beach with "the bulge," Keira teased, winking at all.

Frowning, Charisma tossed the dress on the bed. "The bulge?"

"What else do you expect me to call that man?" Keira asked. "Didn't you see his body in those tight black running shorts? Shit, I don't think he has an ounce of body fat on him. All those muscles bulging out everywhere, and he couldn't take his eyes off of you. I think the man is in love."

Charisma quickly shoved down the tingling of excitement that raced through her body at the thought of Dave having deeper feelings for her. He wasn't interested in her that way. Dave was a very attractive man that liked flirting with her, and she was the kind of woman who enjoyed flirting back. It wasn't ever going to go any further than that.

Don't lie to yourself. You know that you want to see him completely naked.

"I don't know what you're talking about, Keira," she sighed. "Dave is just an acquaintance, and nothing more."

Keira's soft giggles sounded like nails on a chalkboard to her. "You keep telling yourself that, and maybe you'll start to believe that lie."

Taking offense, Charisma folded her arms over her breasts and narrowed her eyes at her best friend. "Are you really calling me a liar?"

A tiny grin pulled at the corners of her friend's mouth making her eyes light up her caramel face. "Hey, don't act you're all upset with me. I'm speaking the truth, and you know it. The second you spotted Dave running towards us on the beach, you got all hot and bothered. I swear I saw your body break out into a sweat."

Embarrassment flooded Charisma's face as Keira's words sunk in, and she realized she wasn't doing a good job of keeping her attraction to Dave hidden. "Umm...so what? I got a little excited when I saw him, but can you blame me? Did you see how he looked in those trunks?"

"Please don't get all defensive on me. Dave might be the one for you like Clinton was for Jenisha and Hayward was for True."

She seriously doubted that the fine-as-hell specimen Dave Turner was thinking about marrying her. Sure, they couldn't keep their hands off each other, but they didn't mean they were on their way down the aisle.

"Why don't you stop trying to play matchmaking, and go get dress? I heard the food in this restaurant is mind-blowing," Charisma said going to the dresser and pulling out a matching underwear set. "I want to get down there early so I can get a good table. You never know. Mr. Right might walk through the door tonight."

"I think we both already know that you've met Mr. Right," Keira accused before she rushed from the room.

Charisma twirled away from the dresser to tell Keira what she thought of her opinion, but it was too late. Her friend was already halfway back to her own room. "Keira doesn't know what she's talking about. Dave isn't the man for me. He can't be," she told herself, throwing her underwear down on the bed.

Was he?

* * * *

"What has put that goofy grin on your face, big brother? I haven't seen that look since your graduation from college. Did you find a woman while you were out on your run?"

Looking up from the clothes on his bed, Dave glowered at his sister standing at his bedroom door wearing a pink sundress with matching sandals. She always found a way to come around when he didn't want her to. "I don't have a goofy grin on my face," he countered, moving away from the bed. "I'm just glad I decided to say yes to this trip. It's just what I needed. I didn't realize how hard I have been working to graduate early."

Brittney made a sound in the back of her throat like she didn't believe him. "Sure, that's the reason it's taking you so long to get dressed. I know you, big brother.

You're trying to impress some woman. You're such a player. You haven't been here twenty-four hours, and you already have your sights set on someone."

He hated when Brittney knew something was going on with him. He couldn't keep anything from his mature-beyond-her-year's sister. "I'm not getting dressed up for anyone. Can't I just want to look nice when I have dinner with my pest of a little sister?"

"Sorry, but you won't be having dinner with me," Brittney exclaimed. "I'm having dinner with a group of other teenagers I met on the beach, and then we're going to a bonfire."

Dave didn't like what he was hearing. Brittney knew she wasn't about to go with a group of strangers that he didn't know. "Whoa...wait one minute. You aren't going out with a group of people I've never met. What in the hell is wrong with you? I don't let you do that back home. Why in the hell will I let you do it here?"

"Dave...you know that I'm a responsible and wouldn't get into any trouble," Brittney complained, tapping her sandal against the carpet. "I'm going to down in the dining room at the same time as you, so you'll see me, and the bonfire is being sponsored by the hotel. There's even going to be police officers there to make sure things don't get out of hand. Why can't I go to this?"

All of it sounded okay, but he still didn't think his baby sister needed to be running around on the beach late at night. "Brittney, I don't mind about you having dinner with the kids, but the bonfire is out. I want you back up here in this room right after dinner."

"That is so unfair," Brittney cried, folding her arms under her breasts. "Why can't you give me an ounce of credit and trust me? Have I ever done anything not to make you trust me?"

That tantrum might have worked on their parents, but she was with him now, and he wasn't going to fall for it.

He wanted her back in this room after dinner, and it would happen. "Sorry, Brittney. If you don't want to follow my rules, then you can throw a fit, and we'll both having dinner here in our rooms." Dave hated the fact that he might not see Charisma again until tomorrow, but he had to keep a close eye on his sister.

"Fine. I'll come back here after dinner," Brittney muttered, still pissed at him, "but I think it's so unfair you get to go out and have fun, and I can't."

Moving around the room, Dave hugged his baby sister even though she didn't return the hug. "I know you're mad at me, but I can't let you go wandering around late at night in Jamaica. It would kill me if anything happened to you. Don't you know I love you?"

Brittney gave him a quick hug and stepped back. "I love you, too," she admitted. "I'm still upset, but I understand, and I promise I'll come back up here after dinner." Planting a kiss on him, Brittney raced from the room with her long blond ponytail swinging behind her.

"Thank God she didn't fight me too hard on that, because I didn't want to miss out on having dinner with Charisma," Dave sighed as he headed to the shower. "She's going to be so surprise when I join her tonight."

For the next two weeks while he was here, he planned to seduce Charisma Miles in ways that she had only imagined with other men. He may not win her over in the next fourteen days, but he would win a piece of her heart and get the rest when they got back to the States. He wasn't going to let her run from him like she had done in the past.

Hayward won over True. Clinton snatched up Jenisha, and he was going to do the same thing with Charisma. She wasn't going to stand a chance against him when he cut loose and let everything out on the table. The last eight years of his life he had been searching for something, and he hadn't known what it was until he saw his friends get married.

Hayward and Clinton had the lives that he wanted, and Charisma was the only woman he desired to have that relationship with. She came off like a tigress, but she was a scared baby cub waiting to be stroked in the right way.

Shit, he hadn't forgotten about that sweet stolen kiss in Jenisha's living room. He had wanted so bad to pursue her, but he didn't have anything to offer her back then; however, now with his college degree and a job at Campbell Construction and Design when he got back home, he was on the same playing field as the men Charisma worked with at that sports agency.

Now he'll be able to take her out to nice restaurants and buy her cute little gifts to seduce her mind and, bit by bit, win over her heart. It felt a little strange to him to be this attracted to someone, but with everything in him, he wanted to get to know Charisma better.

In the past, women smothered him by calling all the time or dropping by unannounced to his house. They tried to make more out of the relationship than there was, but Charisma was the exact opposite when it came to him. She tried to put as much distance between them as she could. She didn't want to see the mind blowing attraction between them. She would rather start a fight with him hoping it would scare him off, but it *wasn't* going to happen.

He had found his partner for life, and nothing was going to make him give her up. Charisma Miles was his the second he spotted her talking to Jenisha inside her classroom, so she better get use to the idea he was going to be her husband.

Chapter Six

"Are you expecting someone to join us for dinner?"

Glancing away from the empty restaurant doorway, Charisma stared into the smiling face of Keira across the table from her. "What are you talking about?" she asked, taking another peek at the door. "I'm not expecting anyone."

"You sure could have fooled me," Keira laughed, tapping her on the back of the hand drawing her attention away from the door again. "With the way your eyes haven't left that door since we arrived, I thought you invited Dave to join us for dinner."

"No, I didn't invite Dave to join us for dinner," she shouted, causing the patrons in the restaurant eyes to swing over in their direction. Charisma lowered her voice. "I don't know where you come up with this stuff. I'm not interested in Dave, so why would I give him an invitation to dinner?"

Picking up a breadstick out of the basket, Keira waved it under her nose. "Oh, I don't know what gave me that idea, but if I had to guess, I would say it has to do with the way your eyes light up when I mention his name."

She disliked how Keira never kept anything to herself, but always let everyone know what she was thinking. "You're wrong. My eyes don't light up when you mention his name. I know nothing about him, and I want to keep it that away," Charisma argued, placing a breadstick on her plate. "We just happen to know each other because Jenisha is married to his boss."

"You're such a liar, Charisma Miles. I know you've dreamt about rubbing sun-tanning oil all over those bulging muscles. Hell, what woman in her right mind wouldn't?" Keira sighed, waving her hand in front of her face.

"You've been to too many strip clubs back home. Haven't I told you to stop fantasizing about rubbing stuff on half-naked men?"

"Hey, we're talking about you and not me. I'm not afraid to go after what I want," Keira countered, taking a bite of her breadstick.

"All right. I'll admit that I've had certain raunchy dreams when it came to Dave. However, it doesn't mean I'm going to act them out," Charisma confessed. "I may come across like a bad girl, but I'm not."

Charisma's eyes widened in shock as Keira choked on the piece of bread in her mouth. She jumped up to help her friend, but retook her seat when Keira waved her back down. She waited while Keira drank some water and regained her composure.

"Where is the real Charisma and what have you done with her?"

"I don't know what you're talking about," Charisma frowned. She hated it when Keira talked in riddles like this.

"Aren't you the same girl that danced on top of a bar when we were in college? Aren't you the same girl that entered a wet T-shirt competition twice and won both times? Those things have bad girl written all over them," Keira shot back, grinning.

Charisma couldn't help but smile as she remembered those things like it was yesterday, and she loved those memories. "Don't forget that I also won the contest for that lap dance from the stripper named 'Thunder' that all the women loved."

"Oh....I had forgotten about that, and I don't know why because that happened at the beginning of this year." Leaning across the table, Keira grinned at her. "You are a bad girl with a capital B-A-D, and that's the reason Dave wants you so much."

Just thinking about Dave wanting her made memories of their secret foreplay on the beach rush back to her, but she quickly shoved it away. It wouldn't to any good to let Keira know that Dave has already gotten to third base with her. She had to make sure he didn't get a home run while she was on vacation in Jamaica.

"What put that look on your face?" Keira inquired, moving back.

"What look?" she asked, reaching for her water with lemon.

"Like you're four years old, and your mother caught you with your hand in the cookie jar."

She took a sip of water then placed it back on the table. "Sorry...can't say I know that look, because I never got caught with my hand in the cookie jar like you."

"Hey, you were the one that dared me to do it when your mother left the room," Keira accused with a grin. "My mother spanked me when I got home. I was so upset with you that I almost stopped being your friend."

"Didn't I make it up to you by giving you my piece of chocolate cake at lunch?"

Keira closed her eyes and placed her hand over her heart. "I do love chocolate cake."

"No one could tell by looking at you. What size do you wear anyway, a two?"

"I wear a size six, thank you very much," her friend answered opening her eyes. "Anyway, I would rather have the rack that you do. I don't come any close to filling out a two-piece like you do."

"Well...I've my mother to thank for that. She's the one I get them from," Charisma laughed as Keira rolled her eyes. "You could always buy some."

"Girl...it's homegrown for me or nothing." Keira stopped talking and stared at something over her shoulder. "Double damn..." she whispered. "It's a shame for a man to be that fine."

"He might be pretty gorgeous, because you don't give any guy your double damn," Charisma giggled as she spun around in her chair and found out who caught Keira's attention. Her heart leaped up into her throat as her eyes connected with Dave's.

His eyes raked boldly over her, and her nipples hardened at his possessive look making her body ache for his touch. He radiated a sex appeal that drew her like a moth to a flame.

While Dave was ogling her, she did a little lusting of her own. A light tan suit was molded to his perfect body, and she could almost catch a glimpse of an off-white sleeveless t-shirt underneath, the kind body builders wore when they were working out at the gym, but it was nicer.

The pants were tailored to fit his massive thighs and accommodated that huge bulge that she knew all too well that was resting there for the moment. Taking a quick glance at his wrist, she spotted a watch. Slowly, she raised her eyes back up to his and realized with a start that he hadn't taken his eyes off her the whole time. It was a little unnerving to know he was watching her while she was checking him out.

Charisma watched in shock as one of the waitresses ran up to him, but he shook his head and pointed in her direction. She knew that he wasn't coming over here. "He can't be heading over here," she muttered more to herself than Keira. "Maybe he's meeting someone at the bar."

"Honey, your Dave is headed right for you, so you better get ready," Keira exclaimed. "I'm pretty sure he's not going to leave until he gets what he wants."

"He's not mine," Charisma hissed, trying to calm down the pounding of her heart. She liked how Keira was so sure that Dave wanted her. Unconsciously, she straightened her dress and touched the sides of her short hair and sat up straighter in her seat.

"He's yours," Keira laughed, reaching for her purse on the back of the chair, "and I'm leaving so I won't be a third wheel. He looks like a man with a plan."

Charisma's hand reached out to stop Keira, but she wasn't fast enough. Keira stood up at the same time Dave reached their table. She couldn't believe her friend was going to make tracks and leave her with Dave like this. Charisma silently fumed while Keira spoke to Dave. *I'll get her back for this.*

"Nice to see you again, Dave," Keira said.

"You, too, Keira," Dave answered then looked at her. "I hope I'm not running you off. I just thought it might be nice to have dinner with two beautiful women. I hate to eat alone."

Keira grinned at her around Dave's huge shoulder. "You didn't run me off. I'm going to eat at the bar. I see a guy over that I want to get to know better. So, you can have my seat and eat with Charisma. I know she'll enjoy the company."

"If you're sure," Dave replied with his eyes still on her and not Keira.

"I'm sure, and you two have fun," Keira answered and moved away, but not before she gave her the thumbs up sign behind Dave's back. Charisma watched her friend stroll away from her with a scowl.

She was going to kill Keira for leaving her like this.

* * * *

Shaking off the scorching temptation that always presented itself when Dave was within twenty feet of her, Charisma watched Dave as he took Keira's seat. The air around them seemed to get hotter the second he sat in front of her. *Was it her, or did his body look extra tasty tonight*?

"How did you know I was down here?" she asked, watching how Dave's muscular frame completely covered the chair. It made her wonder how it would feel to have it above her when they made love….not if they ever made love. Charisma silently scolded herself for not staying focused. She wasn't going to sleep with Dave while she was on vacation, or ever, for that fact. He touched a part of her that she didn't want found.

"I didn't know you were down here, but I was hoping that you would be," Dave smiled. "I really wanted some alone time with you. I'm glad your friend left."

"Why? So we can have a repeat of what happened at the beach?" she asked, hurt. *Great, he was just as bad as the men in her past*. Sex first, and nothing else seemed to matter.

Dave's hand reached out and captured hers before she had a chance to move it. "As much as I would *love* to have my fingers inside your tight, warm, and dripping wet body again," he exclaimed staring directly into her eyes, "I want to get to know you better."

Toffee-colored eyes traveled over her face and searched her eyes while Dave rubbed his thumb over the side of her wrist. "Both times I've been around you, I've come on pretty strong, and I can see why you would say that, but I do want to learn what makes those exquisite eyes of yours light up."

"I'm going to be here for the next two weeks, and I want to spend them with you when you aren't with your friend," Dave continued in that deep hypnotic voice she loved listening to. "What do you say? We can make Jamaica our on little paradise."

"No sex?" Charisma asked. Dave was so disturbing yet fantasizing to her on every level that there was. She wanted to enjoy this trip as much as she could before she had to get back to the real world.

A deep chuckle sent her nerve endings on fire. "I'm not going to lie. I've wanted to make love you for a while now, but it can wait, because I want to get to know the inner you more. So, is that a yes?"

Glancing around the restaurant, Charisma let Dave's words play out in her mind, torn between being that impulsive girl back in her college years or the mature woman she had grown into.

At times like this, that impetuous girl still lurked inside her and wanted her to agree to have an island romance throwing caution to the wind. Yet, the mature career-minded woman didn't want to lose focus and get swept away by the attractive man sitting in front of her.

She already hated she questioned Jenisha about him and found out that he was part Filipino and Greek, which gave him that wonderful natural tan coloring. Why did she have to be attracted to Dave? He wasn't like any of her indifferent relationships in the past that she could walk away from after a few months.

It was like he had a link to her subconscious, because everything that came from his sculptured lips she longed to hear. What he was asking her seemed nearly impossible. Spend the next two weeks around all his muscular perfection and not want to rip his clothes off his body. He already had her wanting him because of his tattoos that covered his arms. The right arm had something of Japanese or Kanji script, but she couldn't quite make out what it meant. His left arm was covered in another Kanji tattoo. In addition to those, he had a flame tattoo on his navel. God, she wanted to lick that so badly that her teeth ached, but she wouldn't do it.

Dave didn't know that one time she had came to visit Jenisha at work and saw him outside working without his shirt. She almost fainted at the dragon tattoo that covered his entire back. Tattoos have always been her weakness since her first year of college. When she spotted one on her history professor's arm when he had taken off his jacket, they had secretly dated each other for about two years. But she broke it off when he wanted to get married, and she didn't. If she remembered correctly, he had transferred away from the college during Spring Break. Now here she was again, years later, lusting after another man with tattoos.

Decisions......decisions...what am I going to do?

She quickly answered Dave's question before she chickened out and lost her nerve. "Okay, I would love to spend the next two weeks with you," she replied, pushing down the butterflies in her stomach. When was the last time she had been this jumpy about spending time with a man? Maybe it was because Dave was chasing her, and it wasn't the other way around. She couldn't be this anxious about doing anything with him while they were in Jamaica. He was like any other man she had dated.

Yeah right...Keep lying to yourself.

Chapter Seven

He couldn't believe Charisma agreed to see him for the two weeks while they were in this gorgeous paradise. All kinds of ideas were running through his mind about the different things he wanted to do with and to Charisma during their stay here, but he had to entice her little by little until she became fond of his plans.

Now, it would he hard for him to divide up his time between her and his sister, yet he would do it. Charisma didn't know this was the first part of his plan to win her over and make her his everything for the rest of her life. She was done dating men that didn't deserve the brilliant woman she was.

Dave wondered how long he could keep his word before his emotions took over and he tried to seduce Charisma into his bed. He knew that she was determined to fight him every step of the way, but he was equally determined to make her a permanent part of his life. It was almost like she imposed an iron-controlled contract on herself not to fall in love with him.

While Charisma looked around the place and tried to hide the desire in her eyes she saw there for him, he ogled the dress that hugged her body. Did she have any clue how that red dress was displaying all of her perfect features?

His eyes landed on her the second he stepped into the restaurant, and he wasn't about to take them off her, either. *I can't believe how hard my cock is for Charisma. I know her, but not well enough to be thinking the rest of my life with her*, he thought as a waitress brought a couple's order across from them. Yet, what scared him the most was the thought of Charisma not being in his life.

The connection he felt for her happened lighting fast, but his feelings for her were real, and he would do everything in his power to win her over. If he didn't, then he would be making a trip back to California, and he would romance Charisma until she realized how good they would be together.

He recalled all the time he laughed at Clinton when he said that he fell in love with Jenisha at first sight. Now he knew what his best friend meant. He wasn't about to let Charisma go, not for anything in the world.

All he could think about was watching her walk down the aisle towards him, making love to her in the shower or any place she wanted in their house, and then seeing her grow big with their first child. Dave promised himself he would get everything that Hayward and Clinton had, if not more, with the goddess in front of him.

"Dance with me," he said standing up, oblivious to the females' stares that were glaring his way.

"What?" Charisma gasped. "Shouldn't we order something first and dance later?"

Moving around the table, he gently tugged Charisma out of her chair and led her out to the semi-crowded dance floor. "If I can't quench the main hunger that I have for you, at least humor me with a slow dance," Dave answered as he pulled Charisma's softness into his arms.

The top of her head barely came to his shoulder, and he enjoyed how she still felt so right in his arms. Pressing her close to him, Dave slid his hand down until it cupped her butt. His fingers caressed it lightly, and he smiled at the moan Charisma tried to hide from him. The light sound made his cock jerk to full attention. Shit, that had never happened with any of his old girlfriends. Dropping his head some, he ran his tongue along the side of her ear and took a quick nibble.

"Hey, we can't be doing this on the dance floor," Charisma hissed, squirming in his arms making his erection painfully harder.

"What are we doing?" he asked, rubbing his hardness against her. Dave couldn't get over how his body constantly knew when she was within twenty feet of him. "I thought the only thing we were doing was dancing."

As much as he didn't want to, Dave moved his hands back up to the middle of Charisma's back then placed a kiss by her cute little ear. "Can't two people just enjoy a slow dance with each other?"

Leaning back in his embrace, Charisma's eyes glanced up at his. "You know what you were just doing isn't considered dancing."

"I honestly thought we were dancing with each other. So if we weren't dancing, do you mind telling me what I was doing?" he asked as another slow song came on.

Sighing, Charisma shook her head at him. "You're trying to seduce me, and I won't let that happen. We're just two old friends having a nice time together."

Charisma was challenging him to kiss her senseless in order to wipe that word 'friends' from her luscious mouth. He wasn't about to be placed in the Friend's Wasteland like she had hoped. After their little rendezvous on the beach, they had leaped way over the friends stage, and he would make sure she wouldn't place them back there.

He bent his head so his mouth was by Charisma's ear and murmured, "Sexy, we were way past being friends this afternoon when you came all over my fingers."

Soft whimpers came from her mouth as she tried to jerk out of his arms, but he tightened his grip on her waist holding her in place.

"How dare you fire that back in my face!" she accused, struggling against him as she tried to get free. "Let go of me."

"I'm not throwing anything back in your face," he exclaimed, dancing past another couple that were giving them odd looks. "I'm bragging that you trusted me enough to let me make you lose control."

"Do you have that ability with other women, too?" she asked.

"You're the only woman I want to make scream my name." The music stopped, and he wrapped his arm around her waist and held her in place as she tried to leave him. "I know you can feel I'm rock hard, and you know that you're the cause of it."

A smile pulled at the side of her full mouth. "It would be hard for me to miss, since it has been poking me for the last several minutes. Do you need help getting rid of it?"

Charisma was an ever-changing mystery to him. She was definitely going to keep him on his toes for the next few weeks. "Don't tempt me, because I'll make record time getting you back up to my room. And I promise you my fingers won't be the only thing in that tight body of yours tonight," he guaranteed. "Are you inviting me to do that?"

"No, I'm not ready for that," Charisma answered, running her thumb over his bottom lip, "but you never know what the future holds."

A growl started low in Dave's chest and worked its way up until it eased from his mouth. "You love tempting me, don't you?" he questioned her as he escorted her off the empty dance floor back to their waiting table.

Pulling out the chair, Dave waited until Charisma took her seat and then he kissed the back of her neck. "Have I told you how gorgeous you look tonight?" he breathed against it.

* * * *

He's killing me. Charisma couldn't think of anything but how it felt when Dave was pressed against her on the dance floor. She was always the strong one when it came to her relationships, but Dave took control when he was around and showed no signs of stopping his relenting pursuit of her.

"No, you haven't told me," she mused as Dave took his seat.

"Well, let me fix that right now." He reached across the table for her hand, and she gave it to him. He sensuously stroked the back of it. "You're the most beautiful woman in here tonight, and I'm proud to be your date."

"I never know what you're doing to say," she said, taken back again by this unpredictable side of him. "How about we order dinner before I do something I might regret?" Like her taking Dave back upstairs and ordering room service after she had got acquainted with every inch of his powerfully-built body.

"Care to share?" Dave asked, teasing her skin with his thumb. "I'll swear I'll try to make all of your dreams a reality."

"Is that a promise?" Charisma asked, licking her lips. "Because there's something I want you to do for me." Lowering her lashes, she stole a peek at Dave from underneath them. The heat that radiated from his eyes almost made her choke on her words.

"Name it, and it's yours."

"Could you please let go of my hand, so I can order something to eat?" Surprise raced across Dave's handsome features before his face closed up, and his warm touched slipped away.

Picking up the menu, Dave flipped it open. He stared at her a few more minutes then dropped his gaze. "So what would you like to eat?" he asked in a cool impersonal tone.

She silently kicked herself for making Dave think she didn't want his touch. On the contrary, she got weak in the knees any time his long, warm fingers rubbed her skin. She hated that she hurt his feelings, and she couldn't let him be mad at her for the rest of the night.

Reaching across the table, she lowered the menu away from his face. "Hey," she exclaimed looking at him. "After we finish with dinner, do you want to go walking on the beach?"

Interest lit up his beautiful eyes. "I can't agree to your request unless I get to hold your hand. I think that's the only way to enjoy the beach with an alluring woman."

Dave is such a charmer, she thought.

Charisma's grin caused her perky nose to wrinkle across the top. "Well, we better hurry up and order, because I love the feel of your hands on any part of my body." Giving Dave a sexy wink, she picked up her menu and scanned over the items.

* * * *

She's so damn beautiful. That's all Dave could think about as he watched Charisma playing in the waves as the water rushed over her bare toes. The warm Jamaican air blew across his bare arms. He had taken his jacket off about five minutes after they got down to the beach because of the weather.

Back at the restaurant when Charisma had suggested he move his hand off her, he hated to admit it, but her words had stung. All he was thinking about was how he couldn't get enough of her and the uniqueness that made her so appealing to him. He wanted to snatch her up and make her his forever, but he wouldn't, because he didn't want to scare her away.

He knew from experience that Charisma was a runner when she got cornered, and he didn't want her disappearing on him again. Easing up behind her, he wrapped his arms around her trim waist. "Do you know how breathtaking you look under the moonlight? You look like a mermaid in the water."

"I think my hair is too short for me to be a mermaid," she giggled, "and I hope you would find me pretty no matter how I looked."

"You're perfect to me. I would find you sexy if you had a mole under your chin with hair growing out of it. Or if your eyes were two different colors and you gained eighty pounds on the body I find so hard to resist. I've dated fitness models, lingerie models, and showgirls, but none of them compare to you."

Pivoting in his arms, Charisma placed her smooth hands in the middle of his chest. "Are you trying to charm me again, Mr. Turner? Or are you trying to get another kiss from me?"

"I would love more than a kiss from you, but I'll settle for that," he said before capturing Charisma's full lips with his own.

He licked at the side of her mouth, savoring the lingering taste of peaches that she had on her dessert. Meowing sounds came from her throat as Charisma stood on her tiptoes and opened her mouth slightly as a silent invitation.

Not thinking twice about the offer, Dave worked his tongue inside the wet haven of Charisma's mouth. Scorching heat burned up his body as her soft pink tongue teased and sucked at his. Hell, it was wonderful to have her back in his arms again. How was he going to be able to let her go after this trip?

Slipping his hands down to her firm ass, Dave lifted Charisma until her toned legs enveloped around his waist. The only sounds on the deserted stretch of beach were the lapping of the waves and the low moans of the couple wrapped in each other's embrace.

Without breaking their hot drugging kiss, he bent his knees and gently laid Charisma down on the wet sandy beach: its coarse texture clung to her skin and his, but that didn't stop him. In his mind, it only added to the fervid of the moment.

He moved his mouth over hers devouring its velvetiness after a few deeper kisses, Dave moved his mouth to nibble at the shell of Charisma's earlobe. Burying his face in her neck, he planted a kiss there while her body twisted beneath his.

"Dave, please don't stop," Charisma moaned, scratching his back. "I want to feel you inside of me."

Closing his eyes, Dave prayed for patience he wanted to grant her wish so bad, but he would keep his word. "Honey, don't do this to me," he groaned, untangling her body from his. "We aren't going to make love yet." He stood up and pulled a stunned Charisma to her feet.

Damn, he hated that he was a man of his word.

"You actually stopped," she gasped, staring up at him while her hands brushed the damp sand off her clothes.

Unable to resist not touching her, Dave ran his fingers down the side of her cheek "Yes, I stopped. Do you want to know why?"

Her eyes were filled with a curious deep longing as her fingers played with the necklace around her neck. "Yes, I want to know why. I know you want me as much as I want you, so why put on the brakes? I'm not against having an island romance with you."

He had no intentions of having only an island romance with Charisma. "You're too special for me to make love to out on a deserted beach," Dave exclaimed, linking his fingers through Charisma's. "Come on, I need to get you back to your room. I don't want Keira sending out a search party for us."

"Keira is probably out somewhere dancing the night away with some good-looking guy. I was supposed to go with her," Charisma informed him as she walked back with him towards the hotel.

His Charisma with another man? He wasn't about to let that happen. Stopping in his tracks Dave tugged Charisma back into his chest. "Tell Keira that you aren't interested in dating any other men while you are here in Jamaica."

For a long moment, she looked back at him, then one eyebrow arched in a silent sign she was pleased with his demand. "Are you really only going to see me while you're here?" Charisma asked with skepticism in her voice. "Are you going to promise me that?"

"No, I can't promise you that."

"Why not?" she demanded with the passion he found so sexy. She moved back from him. "I thought I was the only woman in your life for the next two weeks."

Charisma was jealous and a part of him loved it, but not at the expense of his baby sister. He had to spend some time with her while they were here. If it weren't for her, he wouldn't be on this trip and found a way to talk to Charisma. He owed Brittney at least a few hours each day unless she didn't want him around. He remembered being her age and hating how the adults cramped his style.

Cramped his style? God, he was getting old.

"I didn't come on this trip alone."

Eyes narrowed as Charisma stood even straighter and took a couple of more steps back from him. He could see the huge wall falling into place brick by brick between them.

"You have been making out with me while you've another woman waiting for you?" she hissed at him with disgust in her beautiful voice.

Dave caught Charisma's hand before it made contact with his face. He loved that she was all fired up over this. Shit, he couldn't wait to get all this womanly passion in his bed. It was going to be explosive when the two of them finally came together. "Honey, calm down and listen to me," he laughed as his woman tried to jerk her arm loose. He lightly ran his finger down the inside of her wrist trying to calm down the tigress in front of him.

"Let go of my wrist. I don't want to hear anymore," she snapped, tugging at her wrist again. "I don't have time for a cheat or a liar."

"I can't do that, and I'm neither of those things," he countered then kissed the inside of her wrist. His tongue flickered over the smooth area twice, tasting the sweet essence of her.

Charisma stopped struggling long enough for him to move his mouth to brush his lips against hers. Raising his mouth from hers, Dave gazed into her hurt eyes and he knew he had to fix this misunderstanding and quickly. "I came here with my baby sister, so you don't have any reason to be jealous."

"You did that on purpose, didn't you?" Charisma exclaimed, poking her finger into the middle of his chest. "I shouldn't spend anymore time with you while you're here," she threatened.

"Tigress, I love that you were jealous," Dave chuckled, letting go of her arm. He wrapped his arms around Charisma and spun her back in the direction of the hotel. "How about we see if we can make it back inside with getting into another fight?"

"I wasn't jealous," Charisma denied without a glimpse in his direction.

How he loved this woman. She was definitely sugar, spice, and a pinch of sassy to make her everything he wanted. "Fine, don't admit it, but I will," he said. "I was jealous at the thought of another man kissing you."

Removing his arm off her waist, he held open the hotel room door for her and ran his hand over her tight ass as she went past him. *I could get lost in the perfection of her body*, Dave thought as he strolled into the building behind her.

"Mr. Turner, I don't think you should sneak a feel," Charisma teased over her shoulder, "unless I get to touch something on you."

Chapter Eight

Rock hard in seconds. That always happened to him anytime Charisma talked to him that way. It made him think of slipping in and out of her body with nothing on the bed but one sheet covering the mattress. He wanted her naked for his eyes, so he could gaze down and enjoy every ounce of that sexy body.

Dave wanted to hear Charisma screaming out his name in that sultry voice as her first orgasms of the night hit her over and over. The French didn't call it the little death for nothing. The slow sway of her hips on the way to the elevator captivated him. It was only a matter of time before he held that sinful roundness in his hands as he thrust his cock in and out of her dripping wetness.

Pausing in the middle of the floor, he watched as Charisma smiled at two African-American men as they gave her a lingering look, but he couldn't do anything about it. Charisma wasn't his wife or even his girlfriend. However, the girlfriend thing might change before this trip was over.

"Baby, wait up for me," he yelled, running to catch up with Charisma and drawing the guys attention away from his future wife over to him instead.

"Well, you shouldn't walk so slow, "Charisma teased back, stopping at the elevators.

He loved how her eyes ran up and down the length of his body. It only added fuel to his fire at making Charisma his for the rest of their lives. Now all he had to do was make her stop flirting and running from him. It was like she had this private place she wanted to keep them in, away from the rest of the world.

"With a body like yours, I would have bet that you should be able to move faster than that."

"I can show you upstairs how well my body moves," Dave whispered as the two men who were admiring Charisma finally moved away. "How about it?

"I don't think so."

"Why not?" he questioned, running the tips of his fingers across the swell of her breasts. "I can make it an all-nighter if you want me to."

"Dave, honestly, I can't. I've to get up early and take care of some things, but we could meet up later on."

Groaning, Dave dropped his hand away from her and pushed the up arrow on the wall. "I guess I could spend some time with my sister and make sure she doesn't get into any trouble."

"I would love to meet your sister," Charisma said as the elevator opened.

"I would like that, too," he responded as he stepped inside. "But she's so hard to keep up with since we arrived here. She's always on the go, trying out the different activities that the resort has to offer."

"I don't blame her. Jamaica is a beautiful place. I could get lost in the romance of it," Charisma sighed.

The doors closed with a soft thud, and Dave watched Charisma from the corner of his eye as she punched the number for her floor. With the red flowing dress she was wearing today, she reminded him of an island girl. It hugged every curve making him want to strip it right off her body.

All his old girlfriends had hair that flowed down past their shoulders giving him something to run his fingers through while they had sex. But Charisma's hair was cut short, and it turned him on in ways that he could never imagine. He didn't doubt that he could find that same completeness with Charisma that his buddies found with her wives.

* * * *

Charisma tried not to squirm, but if Dave kept staring at her like that, she wouldn't be responsible for her actions. All she could think about on the way back from the beach was how good Dave's body had felt on top of hers.

She had to stop this before it went past a few hot kisses and stolen touches with him. She couldn't get involved with that hunk and the way he constantly mentally stripped each article of clothing from her body. Whatever happened between her and Dave couldn't amount to more than a hot and steamy affair. It wouldn't do either one of them any good to think about a happily every after.

She stole a peek at the numbers on the panel and saw there were still four more floors before it stopped on hers. In her mind, this had to be the slowest moving elevator in history.

Acting indifferent had become such a deep part of her life that Dave's endless appraisal was wearing her down, but she wasn't about to let him know that. After what seemed like ten minutes, the elevator finally came to a stop, and Charisma let out a sigh of relief. Any more time in these closed quarters with Dave and she might start licking those tattoos that covered his massive arms.

"Here I am," she said, stepping out of the elevator with Dave's towering presence right behind her. She felt the warmth of his body as he walked behind her. "You don't have to escort me to the door." Charisma knew that she couldn't stay a minute longer around Dave, or she was going to invite him in to spend the night.

That thought barely left her mind before another followed. All the tingling sensations that Dave evoked in her body was brought back in full force. She had to get away from him immediately before she ended up doing something that she would regret in the morning.

"Thank you for the date and making sure I got back to my room," she said, spinning around to face Dave.

Bedroom-brown eyes held hers for a spilt second before Dave moved closer to her and let his hot gaze run up and down the length of her body. *Don't do this to me,* she thought as the desire in her body for him leaped to life. *Fight it. Don't give in.*

"I really need to get into my room. Keira has probably already worn a hole in the carpet worrying about me," Charisma stated, trying to get rid of Dave, but her excuse even sounded weak to her ears.

"I'm pretty sure your outgoing friend isn't back yet herself," Dave whispered, inching closer. He reached out and cupped her face in his hands, and ran one of his fingers down the side of her face. "Do you share a room with Keira?"

Kiss me....Kiss me, her mind screamed as Dave's wandering touch made her body even weaker to his seduction. She'd never wanted a man as much as she did him. The wetness of her panties only proved that she was losing her battle with keeping him at arms length.

"No, I've my own room, and we share a connecting door," she moaned as two long fingers disappeared inside the top of her strapless dress. "Please stop. We can't go any further out here in the hallway."

Dave gave her a smile that sent her pulse racing. "So, you finally admit that you want me," he smirked, tugging her top down, her breasts sprung free.

She stuck in a breath as the cool air made her nipples even harder. God, how could someone's smile be as intimate as a kiss?

"I never denied that I wasn't attracted to you," she moaned as Dave's fingers played with her nipples. She pressed her legs together to ease some of the ache and tried to continue. "I just can't act on it."

"Why can't you?" Dave asked as he slid a thick thigh between her legs and dropped his head to lick at her exposed breasts.

Plastering her hands on the wall behind her, Charisma let her mind and body get lost in the feel of Dave loving her body, but she knew she had to stop him before someone came out of one of the rooms. She shook of the web of seduction Dave had wrapped around her and gently pushed him away from her body.

"No, we have to stop before someone sees us." Charisma spun around and tried not to notice the thick erection pressed against the front of Dave's slacks. She dug her key out of her purse and as she started to unlock the door, Dave's hand came down on hers.

"I'm only going to let you run for so long," his hot voice breathed at the back of her neck. "I see a future with you, and nothing will stop me from making it happen."

She wanted to believe him, but Dave didn't look like the commitment type. He was way too charming, sexy, and a gorgeous specimen of a man to settle down with one woman.

"Okay big boy, whatever you say," she said. Removing her hand from his, she unlocked the door. She pushed it open and spun around to face her biggest temptation.

"I really enjoyed our date tonight," she said, staring at his lips. She wanted Dave to kiss her again, but she wasn't about to ask him.

"I did too, sexy," his deep voice answered.

Charisma slowly ran her tongue over her bottom lip hoping Dave would make a move. "Will I see you tomorrow?"

"I'm not for sure," he answered, staring at her mouth before he looked back into her eyes. "I think my sister wants me to go scuba diving with her, but after that I'll be yours for the rest of the night."

Dave leaned down and placed a chaste butterfly kiss by the side of her mouth. She had to swallow down her moan of disappointment. He was toying with her, and she hated it.

"I've to take care of a few things tomorrow, too, so how about we don't make any plans and play it by ear?" she replied, mentally trying to take a step back from Dave.

A large hand shot out and placed itself above her head on the doorframe. Dave blocked her in with his magnificent body. "No, I don't like your suggestion. I'll meet you outside on the patio at seven o'clock. I'll reserve a private table for us to dine at. Is that okay with you?"

How could Dave possibly think she could answer his question with him being so close to her like this? Using her index finger, she traced over the tattoo on his left arm. She didn't miss the curse that left his mouth.

"I don't want to take you away from your sister," she replied. "How about we skip our date tomorrow and reschedule it for another day?"

"No, that isn't going to happen. I want to spend time with you, and I'm going to make that happen even if I have to bring my teenage sister along," he promised by her ear and stepped back. "I should go."

She wasn't ready for him to leave yet. "You don't want to stay for a night cap?" Charisma knew that if Dave entered her room, they wouldn't be having a calm conversation over drinks. Because the second the door closed, their clothes would be coming off and thrown all over the floor. The images of Dave hard and naked in front of her rushed a pool of wetness between her legs, soaking her damp panties even more. She wanted him so bad that her stomach was hurting from holding back.

Dave looked up and down the hallway making sure it was clear before he pressed her back against the open door with his sizzling body. "Don't tempt me. I'm hurting really bad, but I'm not going to take what you're offering me. You aren't ready, and neither am I."

How could he say she wasn't ready? Couldn't he feel how her nipples were poking into his rock-hard chest? Did she have to spell it out for him?

"I want you. I'm ready for you," she whispered as her body hummed with pent-up sexual tension. She trailed her hands down his chest until she cupped his long, thick erection. "I can feel you're ready for me, too."

"Baby, don't do that," Dave grabbed, removing her hand. "You're going to make me forget I just told you no."

"But I can't help it," Charisma moaned. "When I look at you, I see a very handsome man that I want to be with."

Dave let go of her hand and stepped back. "Charisma, I see the same thing, but we aren't going to make love until I've all of you. Sure, I can make you want me; however I want you to need me in your life for the good times along with the hard."

Taking a deep, unsteady breath, she stepped back and stared at Dave with a hint of fear in her eyes. She wasn't looking for a commitment. Why couldn't he understand that?

"I can see that I've shocked you, so I'm going to leave and let you think about what I said. But I'm not going to let you run from what we have. I know we can have the same happiness Hayward and Clinton found with your friends if you only give it a chance." With a sexy smile and even sexier wink, Dave turned around and strolled back to the elevator leaving her alone in the open door way.

What in the hell am I going to do? Charisma thought as she shut her hotel room door.

Chapter Nine

"Now why are you sneaking inside your own room again?" a voice taunted behind her making the hairs on the back of her neck stand up. "You're not going to get grounded for staying out past your bedtime."

Gasping, Charisma twirled around and made eye contact with Keira standing in the middle of the floor wrapped up in a dark blue hotel robe. *Thank God!* She counted her blessings that Dave turned down her offer or Keira would have gotten an eye full. Lord, Dave was turning her into a walking hoochie. She had to learn how to control her impulses better around him. Once his hands or mouth touched her body, all rational thoughts left her mind.

She didn't understand why it happened. For God sake, she was a full-grown woman, not a high school girl with a crush. She was past the stage of leaping in feet first when it came to a relationship, but Dave made her want to have sex naked outside in the rain.

"Are you trying to give me a heart attack?" Charisma accused, brushing the thought of Dave naked to the back of her mind. Coming down the three little steps, she moved further into the room. "Besides, what are you doing in my room anyways?"

Keira shrugged her shoulder and wrapped the robe tighter around her waist. "I shouldn't be asking you, but aren't you feeling a little chilly?"

Chilly....what was Keira talking about? She noticed how her friend's eyes dropped away from her face down to the front of her dress. Her eyes followed the same path that Keira's had taken, and Charisma felt her face grow warm as she noticed part of her breast hanging out. She quickly shoved it back in her dress and fixed the straps back in place.

"Hmmm....looks like you were giving Dave a little peek-a-boo show," Keira teased. "I thought he looked like a man that might like to sample the dessert before the main course."

Shameful....her best friend was just shameful. "Don't start," she warned, heading for the other side of the room away from her pesky friend. She hated when Keira caught her doing something that she shouldn't be doing. "My dress got messed up. Dave had *nothing* to do with it. You know how those spaghetti-strapped dresses can be."

"I sure do, especially when you have a sexy man messing with them," Keira giggled. "They always seem not to stay in place. Large as his hands are, I'm surprised the strap wasn't broken."

Waving her hand in the air, Charisma held back her laughter as she tried to shut Keira up. "Okay, stop picking on me. You know that I have no control when it comes to Dave, so we can just leave it at that." Dropping her hand, she eyed her friend. "I'm surprised you're back this early. What happened to the guy you were talking to at the bar?"

"Don't you recognize a bar companion when you see one?" Keira inquired sliding her hands into the pocket of her robe.

"Bar companion?" Charisma frowned, falling down into the expensive settee that she loved. She could spend hours just relaxing on this one piece of furniture and nothing else inside the entire room. "I never heard of a bar companion before," she answered. Keira was always coming up with something new to tell her.

Taking her hands out of her pockets, Keira tied her robe more snugly around her waist and came over to her.

Occupying the seat across her, Keira slid her legs underneath her body and tugged the robe over her exposed knees. "You know what a bar companion is," she stressed. "Think about it a little more."

Charisma knew she didn't have to think about it a little more because she was totally clueless to what Keira was talking about. She loved how Keira thought she still lived in the same world as her. Since she started working as a sports agent, she was out of the loop when it came to the clubs. Maybe when they got back home, she would go out with Keira more and then she would be able to get her undeniable attraction for Dave out of her system.

"No, I honestly don't. Why don't you enlighten me?" She needed something to get the memory of Dave's lips on her body out of her mind. It astounded her that for a big man Dave could be so gentle when it came to her. He made her feel so protected and safe when she was wrapped in his arms.

Jenisha would have a fit once she found out about her spending time with Dave on her vacation. After he left California and went back to Florida, all Jenisha did was push her to call him for an entire month. Even the times she had went to Florida on business, Jenisha called her at the hotel hinting Dave might like a surprise visit from her. She continually lied and told Jenisha that Dave wasn't her type.

She wouldn't have guessed in a million years that the man she was trying to avoid would be on her much deserved and needed vacation. Jenisha would laugh her head off and call True for her to get a good chuckle at her dilemma, too. How did she get herself into such a predicament?

Lord, just thinking about the night she could have with Dave and all of those cord muscles made her heart skip a beat. No, she had to be strong. Sure, she could flirt with him while they were on the island, but reality would set in the second the plane took off from the ground.

"Have you been listening to me?" Keira asked, drawing her mind away from her persistent thoughts of Dave.

"Sorry. My mind was somewhere else," she apologized. "Can you repeat what your said?"

Clicking her tongue, Keira gave her an I-know-who-you-were-thinking-about look. "When are you going to stop drooling over Dave and get with that hunky man?"

"Keira," Charisma sighed. "Dave is a wonderful guy, but I don't see us going anywhere."

"Why? What's wrong with him?"

"I never said anything was wrong with him," she corrected. "He is just from a different world than me. I don't think we could ever fit into the same circle."

"Don't even play that with me," Keira scolded. "You're looking for excuses not to date that man, and you know it. You've dated guys from every class there was, and you know you have. You're scared of Dave, and that's why you don't want to give him a chance."

Charisma didn't like how Keira was digging deep into her mind. What gave her the right to say she was scared of Dave? She wasn't frightened of him at all, and Keira shouldn't imply that she was.

"What gives you the right to tell me that? The last time I checked, you didn't have a psychology degree," she huffed.

"Don't get all snappy with me," Keira came back without batting an eye. "You know the reason we are such good friends is my honesty. You're here on a breathtaking island for free with a man who hasn't taken his eyes off of you, and you want to throw all of that away. Tell me why you can't enjoy you time here with Dave and not think about anything else?"

Keira was right. She had promised Dave over dinner that she would give them a chance, and now she was already trying to find a way out of it. If Dave had the slightest clue that she was having doubts, he would be back down here in a flash.

"I can't think of a good reason."

"Good, that's what I wanted to hear," Keira nodded. "This is your time and not anyone else's. Leave your job back in the states. You know that it will still be there when you get back."

"Have you forgotten about Lily? That she-dragon wants my job, and she might end up getting it, too, if I don't land some more clients," Charisma grumbled. "You should see how she flaunts herself in front of the men at work."

"Don't worry about her," Keira stated. "Didn't you land Brysen Hagerman? He's one of the top paid athletes out there, and he's yours."

She liked Brysen and his wife. They both were so sweet and had invited her to dinner about a month ago. She had scored big when she heard he wasn't pleased with his last agent. It had taken a little bit of coaxing from her to get Brysen to let her sign him, but it all worked for the best in the end.

"I may have landed Brysen, but Lily is sleeping with the boss. Do you really think he's going to keep me when he's getting lip action every night from Lily?"

"That's Lily's talent, but it isn't helping her get the big-name clients like you," Keira countered. "Give yourself some credit. You're an outstanding agent, and most athletes would be lucky to have you representing them."

Charisma's fingers picked at a piece of thread hanging off the end of her dress. "I wish I had your faith in me. Before I left, Easton warned me that my job was in jeopardy." She was scared. She loved being a sports agent. It was almost second nature to her.

Keira waved her comment off with the back of her hand. "Easton's just mad you didn't give him a taste of your kitty kat."

"Kitty kat?"

"Yeah, you know what I mean - a little chocolate loving. Lily wouldn't have a chance in hell against you if you took Easton up on his offer," Keira exclaimed. "I bet he would have let you be on top. A man of his advanced years couldn't take you being on the bottom. It might give him a heart attack."

Charisma's face wrinkled up like she had a bad taste in her mouth. "Are you trying to make me sick? I don't want him anywhere near my body. God, he has slept with half the women on the same floor as me."

"See? That's what I'm saying. Don't let that old pervert enter you mind, especially when you have a sinfully good-looking walking sex machine panting after you," Keira winked.

Walking sex machine…..? Dave would die if he heard Keira call him that.

"What am I going to do with you?" Charisma laughed, getting up from her seat. "You always know what to say to bring me out of my self-pity."

"Hey, isn't that what friends are for?" Keira asked, rising from her seat. "Now, I don't know about you, but I'm ready to hit the bed. I've a breakfast date in the morning, and I can't have bags under my eyes." After giving her a tight hug, Keira left her standing alone in front of her favorite chair.

"Keira's right. I'm going to make every day of my vacation something special and leave work back at home. I can deal with whatever is waiting for me when I get back."

Spinning around, Charisma headed towards her bedroom pausing by the wall to flip off the light surrounding the entire room in darkness. "Dave better watch out, because he's going to have the best time of his life while he's with me," she promised inside the dark room.

Chapter Ten

"You look way too happy this morning. Does this mean you've a secret girlfriend that I don't know about?"

The humid tropical air blew against his arms as he rested his elbows on the table. Dave ran his eyes across the face that bore no resemblance to his own, despite the fact they had the same parents. At first, he hated having a baby sister, because she always wanted to follow him around everywhere. Now, it wasn't so bad, except when she wore clothes that he didn't think was age appropriate.

He was astounded to come back home from California and find Brittney waiting on his doorstep. On his flight back to Florida, he kept wondering why his parents had called him asking when he would be back home. They hadn't contacted him for over a year and then out of the blue, he got a call from them. He should have known they wanted to dump his little sister in his lap and disappear.

However, Brittney hadn't been a problem for him at all. So far, so good. Things weren't going that bad between the two of them. Sometimes he forgot he couldn't do the bachelor things like he used to, like walk around naked in the house after a shower or drink beer and have poker night with his buddies three times a week.

A part of him did miss that but another part liked having another person to talk to when he got home from work. Despite the fact it usually surrounded teenager girl stuff like music videos and the latest designer handbag that

Paris Hilton was carrying, all in all Brittney was a good sister, and he loved having her around.

"Why aren't you out on the beach trying to work on that tan? I thought you swore to your friends that you would be darker when you came back?" he asked, leaning back in his seat.

Popping her gum, Brittney brushed a lock of her hair off her shoulder followed by her usual eye roll. "Don't try to change the subject on me. I heard how late you came in last night," she grinned. "I know you probably have an island girlfriend. Does she know about Trish back home?"

"Trish and I are just friends," Dave snapped and then lowered his voice at the wide-eyed look that came across his sister's angelic face. "Why would you think that we are anything more?"

"You run to her house every time she calls you. What else would I think but that?" Brittney countered, making another bubble and snapped it with a loud pop. "I know something is going on between the two of you. I hear the hushed conversations on the phone."

"First, stop thinking you know what is going on in my life. You're worse than Mom and Dad when they were trying to get me married off. Trish is only my friend, so let it go."

"Whatever," she sighed and moved on her original question. "So, when do I get to meet this island girl you have hooked up with?"

"Charisma isn't an island girl," Dave blurted out then shut he mouth. *Shit.* He hadn't wanted Brittney to know about Charisma yet. Not with her still on the fence about their relationship. Brittney could be a little overprotective of him sometimes when it came to the women he dated. If she thought a woman wasn't good enough for her big brother, she would find a way to break them up.

"Charisma….?" She wrinkled up her forehead and started to drum her perfectly manicure fingers on the table.

"How did you meet her? Was it on the beach or at the hotel? Is she one of the single women here looking for a man?"

With the somber expression plastered across her face, Brittney almost looked exactly like their mother when she was plotting something he wasn't interested in doing. Laughing, Dave got up from his seat and went around the table. Helping up his sister, he gently pulled her away from their table.

"Stay out of my business and go away. I'll meet up with you later on by the jet skis, and we can spend the rest of the morning together," he said.

"Hey, are you trying to get rid of me because Charisma is coming? Let me stay. I promise I'll be sweet and nice. I'll sit there and not say a word," Brittney swore looking back at him over her shoulder.

"You're lying, and we both know it. Now leave, or I might not let you stay out a little longer tonight," he threatened, wanting to get rid of Brittney before Charisma showed up.

Now wasn't the time or place to introduce his sister to his future girlfriend. Charisma was still too nervous around him to be thinking of her as his wife, but it was going to happen. She just wasn't aware of it yet.

"Are you really going to let me stay out later? There's the party the hotel is going to have in the sunroom that I wanted to go to," Brittney stated, moving so she could look up at him. "Can I go?"

"How long does it last?" Dave wanted his sister to have some fun, but he wasn't going to be fooled by her, either. Brittney was a good little con artist when she had to be. Not in a bad way, but when she wanted or needed something, she almost half of the time found a way to achieve her goal.

"Twelve o'clock," she said.

"No, you aren't going to stay out that late. I'll let you stay until eleven o'clock, and that's it."

"But…," Brittney whined.

"Don't even start that on me or I'll make it ten thirty," he threatened, "and you know I'm not playing with you." Brittney must think he was crazy if she thought he would allow her to stay out half the night. No, she was going to be back in their room way before he was. She wasn't old enough yet to be out that late at night and in Jamaica, at that.

"Do we have a deal?" Dave stuck his hand out and waited.

Brittney popped her gum and tapped her foot against the tile on the patio. "I can't say anything to make you let me stay out any longer?"

Shaking his hand, he waved it in his sister's face. "That's it. Take it, or leave it."

"You know that I hate you," Brittney hissed, shaking his hand and dropping it. She rolled her eyes at him and stepped off the patio, stomping all the way to the beach.

"Give me the strength to handle Brittney and all of her drama," Dave groaned, falling down into his seat at the table.

While he sat there and waited for Charisma to join him for their breakfast date, Dave noticed how all the woman on the beach walked by and took more than a passing glance at him. He knew from a young age that he was a good-looking guy and when he was younger, he used it to his advantage.

His mother would die if she ever found out that her old college roommate had made a pass at him when he was eighteen. She had come into town with her daughter and surprised his mother for a high school reunion the school was having.

All of them had been hanging out for about a week and were having dinner one night and his mother's friend decided to sit by him and placed her hand directly between his legs. Her fingers had done more than a little wandering, but he stopped her flirting before it got him too excited. He already had his sights set on her daughter that kept giving him lustful looks. It hadn't matter that she was twenty-five to his eighteen.

The next day, her mother and his mother had gone into town for something, and he found the daughter sunbathing out by the pool. He volunteered to rub suntan lotion on her back, and they ended up having sex right there on the cement by the pool. He had sex with her three more times before they left and went back home to Alaska.

After that experience, he dated women after women trying to find something more than a good sexual partner and an attractive arm piece. He never went out of his realm for a female. They were always at least five feet seven or taller, long hair that stopped between their shoulder blades, and surgically enhanced breasts to be more eye appealing. For years, he dated those fluff types and was quite happy until the day at Jenisha's school that changed his whole life.

Charisma strolled into Jenisha's classroom looking like the most perfect woman he had laid eyes on. Everything about her screamed at him, and he was the type of man who answered his inner calling. Sure, that first date they tried to go out on turned out badly, but that was in the past.

Captivated wasn't the word he thought about when his mind was on her. No, Charisma had enthralled him from the first moment he learned her name. He was certain that Charisma could give him that same completeness that Hayward and Clinton found with their wives.

"Hi," a pleasant voice said by his elbow. Glancing over the railing, he saw a slender blonde standing there wearing a hot pink bikini. She was just the type he used to date until Charisma came into his life. Now, he wasn't even interested in learning her name.

"Hello," he answered out of courtesy.

"I was on the beach and noticed you sitting over here all by yourself, and I was wondering would you like some company. I've a twin, and we would love to have breakfast with you," the blonde said in a voice that was filled with a hint of something extra being offered.

"I'll have to pass," Dave smiled. "I'm waiting for my date to get here. She should be here any moment." His former co-worker Jim Russell would never believe he turned down the opportunity to spend the day with twins.

"She's one lucky woman. Are you sure I can't persuade you to dump her and spend the day with us?" the blonde offered again. "I can promise you'll have a good time."

"Sorry. I'm already in a relationship, but I'm sure there's another man at the hotel willing to take you up on your offer."

Without saying a word, the blonde whirled and stormed off in the direction of her sister who was waiting for her by a sand pile. Dave let the blonde leave his mind as soon as she walked away. This morning was for him to spend with Charisma over a nice quiet breakfast and that's what he was going to do. If everything went okay, he might even sneak in some dinner plans for tonight.

* * * *

How many times was she going to try to find a way out of spending time with him? Charisma tugged at the silver chain around her neck and stared at Dave talking to the blonde on the other side of the railing. She was positioned in the hallway, and she had an excellent view of him, but he couldn't see her.

She could see that the pin-up centerfold blonde was trying to talk Dave into doing something by the look on her face. She wondered what they were talking about. Whatever it was, he wasn't giving into it, and the blonde left in a huff. The effect Dave had on her was maddening. Her pulse raced and her palms got sweaty anytime she got within twenty feet of him. She had never felt so alive, and it scared the shit out of her.

"You're not a coward. Go in there and have breakfast with him. It's not like he wants you to have sex on the table with everyone watching us." *You know that if he asked you to....you might consider it*, her mind jeered. *Shut up!*

Squaring her shoulder, Charisma wiped her damp palms on the front of her jeans and went into the dining room towards the patio. She was halfway to Dave when he turned in his seat and spotted her. She couldn't help the grin that spilt across her face at the pleasure she saw in his eyes.

"Good morning," Charisma whispered, pausing in front of Dave. *Damn he smells good,* she thought.

"Good morning, gorgeous," Dave said standing up. He brushed past her, making sure she got to feel every rippling muscle on his body. Her body clenched with need to have him, but she shoved it back down. Charisma stood still while Dave proved what a gentleman he was by pulling out her seat.

"Have a seat, and we can order," he suggested, pointing to the chair. "You look very pretty this morning in your white shirt and jeans. Do you know how much I want to squeeze your ass?"

"Is this how you greet all your female breakfast dates in the morning?" she asked, taking a seat.

Dave pushed in her chair and leaned down. "It's better that I said that then acted on my instincts," his hot breath whispered into her ear, shooting shivers down her spine to gush between her thighs.

She knew she shouldn't ask, but she had to. "What were you going to do?"

"With the way those jeans are hugging your perfectly formed ass, I want to slid my hand on the inside and find out."

"Find out what?" she asked, trying to control the heat building up in her body.

"If you're wearing any underwear," Dave answered then moved away to retake his seat.

Chapter Eleven

"Mr. Turner, you're a very bad man," Charisma said, grinning at the look that passed over Dave's handsome face. "Sometimes I wonder if I'm woman enough to handle you and your bad ways."

"Do you want to leave so I can show you how bad I can be?" he asked softly. "I'll make you very happy that you did."

Squirming around in her seat, Charisma fought down the need to say yes. It was going to be hard to say good-bye to Dave after the trip was over. However, if she slept with him, it would make things even harder for her.

"As much as I would love to, I already have plans after breakfast," she replied, taking a menu from the rack on the table.

Dave nodded and continued to stare at her. "Oh, what do you and Keira have planned; shopping, swimming, sightseeing, spa time?"

Peeking over the menu, Charisma fixed her gaze on Dave. "I didn't say my plans were with Keira," she replied then dropped her eyes back down to the breakfast option on the menu.

"What?" Dave took the menu out of her hands and laid it down on the tablecloth. "If you aren't going out with Keira, then who are you planning to spend your day with?"

Charisma ran her tongue across her bottom lip and leaned over the table to get a little closer to Dave. "I don't know if I should tell you."

"Why wouldn't you tell me?' Dave questioned with a hint of worry to his voice. "Will I get upset about it?"

She nodded slowly and grinned. "You might. This person is very sexy. I mean, every time I go out with this person, heads turn to get a second look."

"I don't want you going out with this person. Cancel your plans, and I'll do the same with my sister, and we can spend the day together," he suggested.

Charisma tilted her head to the side like she was actually considering doing it. "No, I can't do it. I really want to spend time with this person today."

Crossing his arms over his massive chest, Dave's mouth blew out several deep breaths, and she could tell he was trying to get his temper under control. "Are you going to tell me about this person? When did you make these plans, because you spent all day with me yesterday?"

"Oh, I made them late last night when I was in bed. As much as I wanted to say no, I couldn't."

Dave unfolded his arms and ran his fingers through his short, spiky hair. "Charisma, how many times do I have to tell you that I want a relationship with you? How can you think about going out with another guy after what we did in the hallway by your room? Did it not mean anything to you at all? Who am I competing with this time?"

She wanted to keep this going on, but she couldn't after seeing at the defeated look on Dave's face. She didn't know that he couldn't take a joke. "Dave, I'm not seeing anyone else but you while I'm here on vacation."

"That isn't true, because after breakfast you're spending the day with someone," he exclaimed, watching her with those dark soulful eyes that she could get lost in.

"Yes, I'm spending the day with someone, but it's not what you think," Charisma denied.

Dave pinched the end of his nose and rolled his shoulders. "How about you tell me what it is then?"

"I'm having a day to myself. Keira is going to the spa for a full body treatment and while you're spending time with your sister, I'm going to do a little sightseeing and shopping for my friends."

"You aren't spending the day with another man?"

"No, I'm going to be all alone on this big huge island all by myself, and I can't wait. There are a few shops that I want to go to. Since I'll be by myself, I can take all the time I want," she grinned.

"You love playing with me like that, don't you?" Dave grinned back, bringing the light back into his wonderful eyes. "Why don't you let me go with you? I don't mind carrying your bags around."

She didn't tell Dave her plans for today so he could swoop in and change all of them. She wanted, no needed, this day to herself, and she was going to have it without a six feet five inches, two hundred and twenty pound bodyguard following behind her.

"No, you're going to spend the day with your little sister, and I'm going to have my own fun," Charisma stated. "We both should be able to spend some time away from each other. I'm not going down this road with you anymore."

Reclining back in his seat, Dave ran his eyes slowly over her body. "Isn't there anything that I can do to help you change your mind? How about a nice backrub, shoulder massage, along with slow lingering kisses on that luscious mouth of yours," he suggested in a low voice. "I'm here to do whatever you want."

That was too good of an offer to pass up. Checking around to make sure the other customers weren't looking at her, she leaned across the table showing off her assets to Dave. "You'll do anything I want you to?" she purred.

"Yeah," Dave said as he eyes gazed away from her breasts and made eye contact. "I'll do anything you want."

Charisma eyes swung to the left and to the right before she leaned over the table giving him a perfect view of her full breasts. His cock twitched and swelled even more in his pants. Hell, this woman was going to have him dying from unrequited need if she didn't stop taunting him with her perfect body.

"You're going to spend the day with your sister. You aren't going to cancel your plans with her. I'm not going anywhere important that you have to disappoint her," she exclaimed then fell back into her chair. "Enjoy the day with her, and we can meet up later on."

"What time will you be back?" Dave asked, hating that she was right.

"I'm not for sure. I always get sidetracked when it comes to shopping. Plus, I promised True I'd bring the boys something back."

Dave's eyes lit up with pleasure. "I can't believe how big they're getting. Clinton brought them to see me the last time he was in Florida, and they were all over the place. They really loved the beach and spent the whole day playing in the sand."

Charisma laughed. "Yeah, they're very active. They are almost three years old, aren't they?" She smiled. "True mentioned that Hayward wanted another baby."

He nodded his head in agreement. "Clinton mentioned that to me, too, but I don't know if he's going to get his wish from the way his brother talked. I think Clinton wants another one, too. He seems to forget that he already has three to Hayward's two."

"I'm still stunned that Jenisha has three when the doctors told her she wouldn't ever be able to have any. I'm so happy for her. I love it when her and True have play dates at my house."

"Seeing how happy True and Jenisha are kind of makes me want a family of my own," Charisma mused. She glanced away from Dave and planted her attention on the people swimming out in the ocean without trying to think about Dave as being the father of her children. She didn't want that kind of relationship with him.

Keira wanted her to stop stressing over all her bad relationships and live in the moment with her time with Dave, but she couldn't. Not with everything that was going on back home with her job. Without landing at least two top clients under her roster, she didn't doubt that Lily would have her job by the end of the year.

"Hey, babe, what has put that solemn look on your face?" Dave asked, placing his rough warm hand on top of hers. "You look a million miles away."

Glancing down at Dave's tanned hand on top of hers, Charisma thought about moving hers away, but his touch was giving her the comfort she craved. "I was thinking about work and other stuff."

"True mentioned to me that you got a new job the last time I was in Montana and asked about you. Do you really enjoy being a sports agent?"

She may not be one much longer if Lily had anything to do about it. "I love my job. It's so much fun signing new guys to my roster. The excitement of working with the men so closely is amazing. A couple of them were leery about working with a woman until I got through to them. Some of them even thought it might go past a business relationship."

"Did it?" Dave questioned, signaling a waiter with his free hand over to their table.

Despite the fact that he tried to keep the jealousy out of his voice, Charisma still heard it, and it placed a warm spot in her heart that she had to fight off. "I never mix business with pleasure," she replied, removing her hand. She picked up the menu and took one last look at it before the waiter made his way to their table.

"So, am I going to be the pleasure part since we aren't working together?" Dave flirted as the waiter hurried over to them.

"It all depends," she flirted back, enjoying the natural chemistry between her and the hunk seated in front of her. God, she was having such a good time with Dave. It was going to hurt so damn bad when it all came to an end. She would go back to her life in California, and Dave would go back to Florida and do whatever he was doing.

"Does it all depend on how many times I can make you scream out loud with pleasure when my hands are on or in your scrumptious body?"

Charisma opened her mouth to answer Dave, but quickly changed her mind when she saw the waiter coming their way. "I'll deal with you later, Mr. Turner," she threatened with a smile.

"Not if I get to you first," Dave retorted with a smile of his own as the waiter paused by the table to take their order.

* * * *

Pushing her empty plate away, Charisma stretched her arms above her head and savored the warm air and the sounds of the ocean coming towards her and Dave. She could stay like this all day, but she had things to do and places to go. Keira was out and about on her own like the adventurous woman that she was. So, she was going to take a couple hours for herself.

"I can't keep eating like this, or I won't be able to wear any of the clothes I have back home," she groaned, bringing her arms back down.

"You know you're sexy. So, why are you worried about gaining weight? With a body like yours, it will fall in all the right places making it harder for me to resist you," Dave complained. "I have a hard enough time as it is keeping my hands off that perfect ass of yours."

She loved how Dave constantly praised her, but she couldn't let it go to far. The first time she saw him in Jenisha's classroom, she thought he was a bad boy, and he proved her right by kissing her at Jenisha's house. It took a long time for her to push the memory of his thick erection pressed against her out of her mind. If he was that warm and hard through layers of clothes, she could only imagine how good he would feel inside of her. *STOP IT!!!*

Charisma shook that naughty thought her from mind. How could she keep Dave at arm's distance when she was thinking about stripping him naked? She wanted to learn more about the tattoos that covered his massive body. Maybe he would even let her lick a few of them.

"What are you thinking about, and can I join in the fun?"

Blinking a couple of times, Charisma grinned like a well-fed Cheshire cat at the man positioned in front of her with his elbows on the table. She could see a few of his tattoos peeking out from underneath his white T-shirt.

"I was just daydreaming," she sighed with a wave of her hand. "It's nothing that you would be interested in."

"Why don't you allow me to be the judge of that?" his smooth voice challenged.

"Sorry, big boy. I can't do that," she said, standing up from the table pushing the chair in. "I'm going shopping, and you need to meet your sister."

Dave followed her same movements as his large frame stood up from the table. "I don't like you wandering around the island all by yourself," he frowned. "I still think I should go with you. I can go find my sister, and the three of us can make a day of it."

Charisma moved towards the inside of the restaurant with Dave's comforting warmth at her side. She wanted this time to herself, and she had to make him understand that. She noticed how every single woman they passed by stopped eating to stare at her man? *Her man...*when did Dave become hers? She stiffened at her thought.

"I hope you know that I don't care if they are ogling me," Dave's sinful voice whispered down by her ear. "You're the only woman I want."

"Are you telling me that there isn't some woman waiting for you back in Florida?" she shot back as she sauntered out of the restaurant into the hallway. Charisma was almost half way down the hallway when she realized that Dave was no longer beside her. Twirling around, she spot him back by the wide doors that led into the restaurant's eating area. "What are you still doing way back there?"

He quickly closed the gap between them and pulled her into his arms. "Charisma, I swear that there isn't any woman waiting for me back home."

She wondered why Dave was acting so strange all of the sudden and wanted to ask, but the masculine scent of his cologne was wreaking havoc with her body. She had to get away from him before she did something crazy. "I better go. I have a lot of shopping to do." Charisma tried to move out of Dave's powerfully corded arms, but he wasn't letting her go.

"I think I need something to tide me over until I see you again," he confessed, tipping her head up with his knuckles. The firm pressure and light stroking of his tongue against the side of her mouth caused her to open her mouth for his silent request.

His kiss was surprisingly gentle, despite the power she felt pressed against her body. Wrapping her arms around Dave's neck, she deepened the kiss with a hunger that stunned her. Growling deep in his throat, Dave's large hands cupped her ass and pushed her harder against the erection poking at her stomach.

"I need you so fucking bad," his lips brushed against hers as he spoke.

"I know, but we can't," she breathed back into his mouth as she moved her mouth off his. She gazed up into his eyes. "I don't want to rush into anything."

"I understand, but it doesn't mean I like it," Dave complained and gave her another quick peck on the mouth. "Stay out of trouble, and don't flirt with any men." He turned on his heel and strolled away from her towards the front of the hotel.

"I don't flirt," she yelled at Dave's back. But the only response she got was his deep laughter as he continued to move away from her.

Chapter Twelve

Pushing her dark sunglasses on top of her head, Charisma allowed her body to blend in with the rest of the vacationers sauntering along the sidewalk towards the eye-catching shops while she debated on which one she wanted to visit.

The relaxing warm salt air brushed across her bare arms like a lover's caress, allowing her to take in the colorful hand-painted signs that hung from the shops windows perfectly placed to draw in a tourist's attention.

Adjusting the leather purse on her shoulder, Charisma ventured into the store that displayed cute hand-craved statues that True had mentioned to her the night before she left for her trip. True wanted her to see if she could find some kind of statue for the new collection her husband started about two months ago. Hayward was looking for a certain piece. He was having a hard time finding it in Montana, so True decided to enlist her help.

Inside the store, she wandered up and down the aisle hoping something would catch her attention. She loved shopping for herself and other people. It gave her such pleasure to see her friend's eyes light up after she had given them the perfect gift. Yet, today it didn't seem like she was going to hit the jacket. That was such a shame, because this place had so many cute things, but none of them were for her. She was turning to leave when the sales clerk left from behind the counter and came up to her.

"Ma'am, can I help you find something?" she asked with a faint island accent. The sales clerk's braids pulled back in a tight ponytail displayed her high cheekbones and her slightly doe-like eyes.

Charisma tried not to feel old as the word 'ma'am' settled into her mind, but instead smiled at the young woman. "I was looking for a gift to buy my friend so she could give it to her husband as an anniversary gift. However, I don't see what she wanted." She turned to leave, but the girl stopped her.

"Don't leave. We have a lot of new items in that back. We just haven't had the extra time to bring them out here. I was going to work on doing that this morning," she said. "Is there a certain piece in particular that you wanted?"

Charisma seriously doubted that this shop had want True wanted, but she would ask anyway. Maybe if she couldn't find anything for True, she might be able to get something for herself.

"I've a picture that I can show you," she replied, digging the photo out of her purse that True had emailed her the day before she left for her trip.

"Here it is," Charisma said, handing the girl the piece of paper. "My best friend's husband is looking for it. She said that Hayward told her it's done by an artist that lives here."

Taking the picture from her, the sales girl glanced at it and ginned. "Don't go anywhere. I think I might be able to help you and your friend." Spinning around, the girl hurried away from her into a room at the very back of the brightly decorated shop.

"I guess I don't have much of a choice since you have my picture," Charisma sighed under her breath as her eyes drifted over the scarves that hung from the walls. She wondered what they were used for.

A white one with gold trim around the edges towards the bottom of the wall caught her attention. She had a white dress back home that would go perfectly with it.

Charisma moved her way around two racks of clothes over to the scarf.

Taking it off the rack, she held it up to the window and watched how the sun played with the gold woven into the silky fabric. "It's gorgeous," she whispered, folding the material over her arm. Charisma reached for a dark red scarf when a sight outside the window caught her attention making her hand stop in mid-air.

"It can't be him," she said, moving closer to the window. "Could I have done something in another life time to get this lucky? Ross Ferguson isn't standing less than twenty feet in front of me signing autographs."

Ross Ferguson was the star quarterback for the Providers. If she wasn't mistaken, he just fired his sports agent a month ago because he was stealing money from him. If she signed Ross, or at least got a chance to get a meeting with him, Charisma knew she would land him as her client.

All the sports announcers called him the golden boy of football, and he had been getting offers from agents left and right, but he wasn't signing with any of them. Even Lily had tried to set up a business lunch with him, and he turned her down. *Sweet Jesus,* this could be her chance to get her top-notch level back at her job. She just had to catch him before he left.

Placing the scarf back on the hook, Charisma rushed out the door and across the street, silently praying that Ross wouldn't blow her off. "Mr. Ferguson, may I speak to you for a few minutes?" she said, stopping at his left side as his last fan walked away. She wondered could he hear how loud her heart was pounding in her chest as he turned to face her.

"I'm sorry to bother you, but my name is Charisma…."

"I know who you are, Miss Miles," Ross southern voice interrupted, shocking her.

"You do?" she whispered, totally taken back.

"Yes. I've heard a couple of players talking about you in the locker room a few months back, and then a couple of the guys pointed you out to me after one of our games. You were having dinner with another woman and twins boys."

Charisma couldn't believe that Ross remembered her. She had dinner with True a little over four months ago. It was one of those times she was trying to work up enough nerve to ask about Dave, but chickened out at the last minute. Why would he even let that stay in his mind?

"I'm going to be honest. I'm very surprised that you know who I am."

Light blue eyes shined at her as Ross gave her the smile he usually flashed for the cameras after winning a game. "It's my business to know all of the sport agents out there, especially the ones who want a piece of me."

Was that an insult, she wondered.

"Mr. Ferguson, I never said that I wanted a piece of you. I only wanted a moment of your time. I thought maybe we could talk about you letting me sign you. I know that I haven't dealt with anyone as famous as you, but I know that I can be a wonderful additional to your team."

"I don't know too many guys that have a woman sports agent," Ross stated. "However, I do know the guys you have, and they speak very highly of your skills."

Charisma couldn't keep the smile off her face. She didn't have a lot of clients like some of her co-workers, but the ones she did have made her job so enjoyable. "Does that mean you'll let me talk to you?"

"I don't know. I had a meeting with that Lily Kane, and she wasn't what I wanted at all in an agent."

"Lily and I aren't the same," she snapped. "We hold totally different business styles."

"Am I sensing a little competition between the two of you?" Ross laughed.

Charisma scolded herself for losing her temper in front of a potential new client. Her outburst wasn't going to gain his trust or loyalty, and she needed both to sign him. "I apologize. I shouldn't have lost it like that."

"Don't worry about it. It shows me that you have passion. Maybe the kind of passion I've been searching for in the person to represent me. How about we have dinner, and you can tell me about yourself?"

Dinner? Charisma couldn't have dinner with Ross. She already had dinner plans with Dave, but this was her career. She might not get another opportunity to meet someone of this notoriety again. She would just explain to Dave and hoped he understood.

"Is your silence a no?"

"No. I would like to have dinner with you," Charisma assured Ross. She wasn't going to miss out on this once-in-a-lifetime opportunity. "I think I can convince you over a nice meal to let me become your agent."

Ross chortled. "You sound very confident," he said, staring down at her with a pleased look in his light eyes.

"I'm very good at my job," Charisma smiled back with confidence. "Give me a chance to prove it to you."

"I'll see how good you are over a nice dinner," he said. "Do you want me to pick you up, or should we meet some place?"

Charisma hated that she couldn't have her date with Dave. But after she explained things to him, he would understand and accept an IOU for their date. Dave knew how much her job meant to her.

"How about we have dinner at the hotel I'm staying at? The food there is wonderful, and I think it will be a good place for us to meet."

"Sounds like a date to me," Ross stated then winked at her. "I think I'm going to enjoy getting to know you better."

She had to set a few things straight with Ross before he got the wrong idea about her. "Mr. Ferguson, this is a business meal, not a date. I don't have personal relationships with any of my male clients. It's strictly business, and nothing else."

A look flashed over Ross's attractive features that she couldn't read. "Well, you're full of surprises, Miss Miles," he replied. "Give me the name of your hotel, and I'll be waiting for you in the hobby thirty minutes before the hour."

"Alright," Charisma agreed and told Ross the name of the hotel where she was staying. "I'll see you there and hoping you'll like what I have to say." She gave Ross a quick wave before she hurried back across the street to the shop. She trusted that Dave wouldn't be too upset with her for having to cancel their plans.

* * * *

"You've been in such a good mood since we came here. Do you have a secret girlfriend that I don't know about?" Brittney teased, stealing a French fry off his plate.

"Why are you so nosy?" Dave asked, shoving the half-full plate of fries at his sister. "Do I ask you about all the boyfriends you have back at home?"

Brittney frowned at him. "You know I don't have a boyfriend back at home, because they are all scared of you. The last guy that asked me out changed his mind after he saw you pick me up after school."

"Can I help I don't want any losers dating my only sister?" Dave asked then took a sip of his drink. "I've to look out for you until Mom and Dad get back."

"Stop changing the subject. Do you have a girlfriend? I know that you have been coming in pretty last these last couple of nights. Are you making sure I'm not going to have any nieces or nephews running around?"

He hated when Brittney teased him like this. What was she doing asking him these questions anyway? She was the teenager, but he was the adult. "I don't think that is any of your business, little sister."

Pouring an excessive amount of ketchup on her fries, Brittney shoved two in her mouth. "Don't try to act all innocent on me, Dave. I know you're not all pure and innocent. I heard the story about how you slept with mom's best friend's daughter all of those years ago," she said around the food in her mouth.

Dave's voice was cold when he asked, "Who told you about that? It was years ago and something you shouldn't know about." Hell, he couldn't stand it if Charisma found that out about him. He was young and reckless back then.

"Oh, I heard Mom talking about it to some woman on the phone a while back. She didn't even know I was outside the door listening," Brittney grinned. "So, my big brother was a player."

"Brittney," he growled.

"Okay, I'll stop teasing you," she grinned, grabbing another fry. "Are you going to tell me about this woman? Isn't her name Charisma?"

Brittney wouldn't leave him alone for the rest of the day if he didn't tell her what she wanted, and he didn't want her making him late for his date tonight. "I met Charisma while I was in California working on that school job with Jim. She's best friends with True's friend, Jenisha Campbell."

"I know who True and Jenisha are. They have the cutest kids," Brittney interrupted.

"Well, I asked her out a couple of times while I was in California," Dave continued like his sister hadn't said a word. "It didn't work out all that well, but I wasn't about to give up. I was thinking about contacting her again after this trip."

"But something happened to stop you, didn't it?" Brittney questioned, waving a soaked French fry at him then shoved it in her mouth.

"Yeah. She ended up here with me. She wanted a vacation from her job and decided to take a trip with her best friend."

"My brother has a girlfriend, and her name is Charisma," his sister teased, wiggling her eyebrows at him.

"Will you stop acting silly?" Dave scolded, wanting to be mad at Brittney, but ruined it by breaking out into laughter. He loved his sister had this goofy side to her. "She isn't my girlfriend yet, but I'm working on it. Hopefully, she'll want to see me again after we leave Jamaica."

"Does she live in Florida?"

God, he wished that Charisma did. "No, she lives in California," he sighed.

"Seriously," Brittney said. "You're trying to have a long-distanced relationship?"

"Yes, if Charisma agrees to it. We only have a few days left on this trip, and I want to spend them with her. I'm going to ask her tonight about the long-distance thing," Dave replied, more than nervous about what Charisma's answer would be.

"Do you think she'll say yes?"

"I hope so," he replied.

* * * *

Charisma fixed the black skirt and matching short sleeve jacket one more time before she ran her fingers through her hair. It was longer than she usually kept it, so when she got back home, she was going to have it cut again. She didn't have the time or energy to keep up with long hair the way True and Jenisha did.

Smoothing her hands over her front, she checked out her reflection from the back making sure there wasn't any visible panty lines. She had to make a good impression on Ross so he would at least think about signing with her. Sure, she was trying to look nice to hold his attention. However, when it came down to it, her track record would speak for itself.

It might be harder than hell for her to sign Ross Ferguson since he was already an established player, but she had to try her best. The other players she had were a lot younger, and she hoped they stayed with her.

Lily was always telling her to offer some kind of incentives like luxury gifts, insurance, cars, and anything else that seemed pricey and too-good-to-be true. But she wasn't like that and never wanted to become like Lily. What she had to offer was more important. She was giving her potential client a valuable asset. One hundred percent of her skills and loyalty, and the only thing she asked for in return was their respect.

Charisma wanted her men to believe in her and trust that she would do the best thing for them and their careers. She had heard that most sport agents should have at least a dozen or more clients, and she was far short of that. Yet, the ones she did have were bringing in enough money that she didn't have to worry about paying her bills.

"Have you talked to Dave yet?" Keira asked, making her glance at her sprawled out on her bed through the mirror.

"No, I haven't. You know that I called him, but he still must be out with his sister. I'm hoping to catch him before Ross gets here."

"You're so lucky. I'm jealous you've having dinner with Ross Ferguson. Can't I go along? I promise I'll be good," Keira said, sitting up in the bed.

Charisma shook her head. "Nope. I can't have you drooling all over the poor guy. I'm trying to get him on my side. Can't do that with you there staring at him all night."

"I wouldn't drool over him all night," Keira denied. "Maybe only for the first twenty minutes."

"How did I end up with such a crazy friend?" she asked, turning away from the mirror. "Does this outfit look professional enough?"

"It's sexy, but it also screams 'I'm a business woman tonight and nothing else.'" Keira replied, getting off the bed. "Let's go girl. I want to get a good table downstairs so I can stare at Ross from a distance."

Charisma moved around Keira picking up her purse and a proposal off the table by the loveseat. "You have no shame. I'm trying to get more clients on my roster, and you're thinking about getting a man."

"Can you blame me? Ross is a hottie, and he's single," Keira sighed, brushing past her to open the hotel room door. "I'm just waiting to see how well your Dave takes the news."

"Dave isn't 'my Dave', so stop saying that," she groaned following Keira out the door, slamming it shut behind them.

"Oh, you're saying that now, but both of us know that it's a lie." Keira kept walking in front of her until she got to the elevators. Pushing the down button, she pivoted to face her. "The only thing I've to say is when you break your date with him, be gentle. I can tell you have the ability to break his heart into a million little pieces."

"If you weren't my sorority sister, I would kill you within an inch of your life," Charisma teased back as the elevator's doors open, and Keira sauntered inside.

"Oh, I know you love me."

"Hmmm, I might have to think about that one," Charisma pondered, joining Keira in the elevator and pushed the down button.

Neither one of them talked as they waited to get to their destination and when the doors opened, Charisma was shocked to find Dave standing on the other side. Stepping out of the elevator, she planted a kiss on his mouth and moved back.

"I didn't expect to see you down here," Charisma said smiling at him.

"Am I late for our date?" Dave asked, looking down at her clothes. "You're look stunning by the way. Just let me go upstairs and get ready." Dave started to move past her, but she moved in his path blocking it.

"I'm not having dinner with you tonight. I have to cancel our plans."

"Why?" Dave asked, frowning. "I thought we set these plans up over breakfast."

"We did, but something came up, and I have to cancel them. Please understand," she said then looked towards the entrance door.

Dave followed her eyes and swung them back over to her. "Are you waiting for someone?"

"Yes."

"Who?" he demanded in a low voice.

"Dave, it isn't what you're thinking," Charisma assured him. "It's a business dinner."

"Charisma, who are you meeting?" Dave asked again, a little louder this time.

"I'm meeting with a potential client," she answered quickly. "If I can sign him, it will help me immensely when I go back home. I can't afford not to have this dinner."

"How long will it take? Do you think we can at least have dessert together?" Dave asked, pulling her into his arms.

"Okay. I can't take much more of you two," Keira groaned moving around the couple then stopped. "I'm not having dinner with anyone Dave, so you're welcome to join me. We can spy on Charisma and Ross Ferguson from a safe distance."

"You're trying to sign Ross Ferguson?" Dave said, shocked. "Isn't he the top quarterback in football at the moment?"

Easing back from Dave, Charisma tried to calm down her racing nerves. "Yes, he is, and I'm scared to death that he won't like what I've to say."

"Baby, you're intelligent, beautiful, and have an honesty about you that draws people," Dave stated. "If Ross Ferguson doesn't sign to your roster, than he's an idiot, and you don't need him."

Charisma tried to stop the sensations that swelled up in the middle of her chest, but she couldn't. How did Dave always find a way to make her feel better about herself and her abilities as a business woman?

"Thank you," she whispered.

"You're welcome," Dave responded. "Now take a deep breath, and show Ross what you got." He planted a soft wet kiss on her mouth then moved back.

Turning away from her, Dave looked at Keira, "Since you invited me to dinner, does that mean you're paying?"

Keira's hazel eyes shot over to her. "Can you believe he just asked me that?"

Smothering down a laugh, Charisma said, "Well, he's right. You did invite him to dinner, Keira. It's only right that you pay for the meal."

"The two of you deserve each other," Keira snapped at her, but Charisma could see the sparkle in her friend's eyes.

"Does that mean you're going to pay for my meal?" Dave asked placing his arm around her best friend's shoulder. "Because if you are, I think I might order an appetizer, too."

Keira brushed Dave's off her shoulder. "Charisma, you better work fast, or you're boyfriend is going to have me washing dishes to pay for this meal."

"No, I wouldn't," Dave interrupted winking at her. "I would wash them and let Keira dry."

Shaking her head, Charisma wondered if would Keira be able to handle Dave and his wild sense of humor while she had her business meeting. "Dave, you better stop picking on Keira, or I won't try to have dessert with you."

"Will you have dessert up in my room?"

"It all depends."

"Depends on what?" Dave questioned in a rich masculine voice, drawing her to more to him than she wanted.

Charisma forgot all about Keira being next to Dave as she got lost in the dark richness of his brown eyes. "On how well you act tonight while I'm at my business meeting. I don't want you staring across the room making Ross nervous."

"I promise I'll be on my best behavior," he swore, holding up two fingers.

"I didn't know you were in the boy scouts?"

"There's a lot of you don't know about me, but I'm planning to fix that," he replied. "I hope your dinner turns out the way you want. At least think about me once or twice."

"So do I," she agreed looking at Dave then over at Keira. "Please keep him out of trouble. He can be a real charmer when he wants to be."

"I bet he can," Keira agreed. She grabbed Dave by the arm and pulled him towards the restaurant door. "Come on, Turner. I want to get a good seat."

Charisma watched Keira lead Dave into the restaurant and wondered if her friend knew that Dave allowed her to do that to him. If he didn't want to move, there was no way in hell Keira could have budged him.

Chapter Thirteen

"Tell me about Charisma. What are her likes and dislikes? What does she look for in a man? Do you think I've a chance with her?"

Keira took another bite of her Curry Chicken enjoying the hint of garlic that hung to the juicy meat. She watched Dave while he waited for her answer. He was glancing over her shoulder at Charisma and Ross. Dave hadn't taken his eyes off them since they walked into the restaurant.

"Charisma is a very complicated woman. Her tastes are constantly changing. She never dates the same kind of guy twice."

"Does that mean you don't think I've a chance with her?" he questioned, dragging his eyes away from Charisma long enough to look at her. "She already knows that I want more than just friendship."

"Dave, Charisma and I have been best friends since college, and I still don't know how her mind works," Keira paused at the disappointed look that passed over Dave's handsome face. "However, I do know that she finds you very attractive and funny. She has never talked about a guy as much as she does about you."

Happiness lit up the dark brown eyes in front of her. "I think Charisma is the most amazing woman I've ever had the pleasure of meeting. The second I saw her in Jenisha's classroom, I wanted her to be mine. I think I came on a little too strong the first time."

She swallowed down a giggle and ate another piece of her meat. Keira couldn't tell Dave what Charisma thought about him and that kiss. She talked about it for days. Her friend was falling for the huge guy sitting in front of her and was fighting it with every breath in her body. Dave Turner wasn't the guy she pictured Charisma with for the rest of her life, but life had a way of playing tricks on you.

"You're in love with her, aren't you?"

"I believe my feelings for Charisma are moving in that direction," Dave answered, folding his arms on the table. "I see what my buddies have with their wives, and I want that."

"With Charisma?" she questioned, pushing her plate to the side of the table.

"Yes," Dave answered without taking a second to think about it.

"I think the two of you make a gorgeous couple, but Charisma is going to fight her feelings for you. She isn't used to a good man. Most of her past boyfriends weren't all that creditable, if you know what I mean. I love her to death and don't want her hurt."

"I would never hurt Charisma. I only want the best for her, and I think the best is me."

Crossing her arms over her chest, Keira leaned back in her seat. "True and Jenisha aren't going to believe this."

"Believe what?"

"I think you lasted about the same amount of time that Hayward and Clinton did when they first laid eyes on them."

"I wouldn't laugh if I was you," Dave warned her. "I laughed at them, and then Charisma came into the picture. I couldn't think of anything else but her."

"I'm not looking for a relationship. I've too much going on back home to even think about becoming involved with a guy," she sighed, sitting back up.

"Anything I can help you with?"

Keira was touched that Dave wanted to help her, and they were virtually strangers. "No. My father hasn't been doing well. He's feeling better now, but we don't know how much longer he'll be up and moving around."

"Well, I hope he gets better," Dave said with genuine concern.

"I do, too, but it doesn't look like he will," Keira replied, blinking back sudden tears.

"Did the doctors say how much longer he has?" Dave inquired, handing her a napkin off the table.

"Maybe two months, if we're lucky." She took the napkin and wiped her eyes. "Now, I wasn't supposed to start talking about my Dad. You wanted to know about Charisma, and the conversation got turned around to me."

"Charisma would want you to get it out. Does she know about all of this?"

"Yeah. That's the reason she invited me on this vacation. She wanted me to get my mind off things and be ready for the worst when it happens." Keira looked over her shoulder at Charisma. "She's really a wonderful friend. I'm close to True and Jenisha, too, but not like I am with Charisma."

"Charisma is one of a kind," Dave agreed. "Hopefully, one day soon, she'll be my one of a kind."

Keira dabbed the rest of her tears away and swung back around in her seat. "I had my doubts about you, but you proved me wrong. You're a wonderful guy, and I hope you end up with Charisma. She deserves someone like you."

"Thanks," Dave smiled. "How about you help me decide what dessert to order for Charisma? I want something that will make her fall in love with me."

"Chocolate," she responded knowingly.

"Chocolate?"

"My best friend is in heaven when there is chocolate around. So, if you order that triple chocolate cake on the menu and have it upstairs waiting for her, she'll love you."

Snapping the menu shut, Dave grinned at her and signaled a waiter over to their table. "I owe you for this."

"No, you don't," she denied with a wave of her hand. "I only want Charisma to be happy, and I think you're the man to do it."

"Thanks for being on my side," Dave said, his firm lips pulling into a wide smile. "Now all I've to do is get Charisma to agree with both of us."

"She will. Just give her time," Keira encouraged."

"I will, because Charisma is the woman I want to spend the rest of my life with," Dave confessed then looked over her shoulder.

* * * *

Charisma was having a hard time paying attention to what Ross was asking her, because she couldn't take her eyes off Dave. He looked so damn sexy in his black T-shirt and jeans. Even from this distance, she could make out the muscles bulging underneath his shirt. Jealousy was eating away at her. She didn't know what he and Keira had so much in common, but the two of them hadn't stopped talking since they sat down.

Her jealousy had no basis at all. Dave wasn't her boyfriend or anything, but he was a flirt and so was Keira when it came to the right guy. Her best friend had that untapped sexiness and only brought out a certain times and tonight it was shining bright.

"Do you know those two people?" Ross inquired, looking over his shoulder at Dave and Charisma. "You haven't taken you eyes off them all night."

"I'm so sorry," Keira apologized, taking one final look at the couple. "Yeah, I know them."

"Ex-boyfriend?"

"No."

"Guys who wants to be your boyfriend?" Ross grinned.

"Why? Don't you think they're a couple?" Charisma asked before she could stop herself.

"I can see their reflections through the mirror behind you, and that guy has turned around and stared at you at least six times tonight. He's acting like a man who very interested in taking things further with you."

"You're very insightful," Charisma exclaimed.

"I know how he feels," Ross shrugged. "There's a girl back home that I want to date, but she isn't fond of the pressures that comes with dating me. She's a homebody, and, well you know, I can't be that with my career."

"How about we both talk about something different?" Charisma suggested, wanting to keep her dealings with Ross business and not jump the invisible line to personal.

"I can handle that. Is now the time when you're going to tell me why I should sign a contract with you?"

"You bet it is," she grinned, but a little concerned that Ross might not like what she had to offer.

"Let me hear what you have to say," Ross said, launching the ball back in her court. "I've a lot of offers since the word got out I'm looking for a new agent. Even a woman from your own company tried to sign me, and I turned her down."

"For the last time, I'm not Lily. I haven't and wouldn't try to use anything but my intelligence to sign you."

"Fair enough," he stated in a skeptical voice, making her even more nervous than she already was.

"Ross, I think you and I would make a wonderful team. You're a talented man that deserves the best agent side by side with you to further your outstanding career.

"The contract I offer is for two years. With me, there's a clause that states that either one of us can terminate the contract after one month. Loyalty is very important to me. I can't have anyone with me that isn't there one hundred percent. If I get lucky enough to sign you, I know without a doubt before the ink is dry on the paperwork, other agents will be calling you offering a too-good-to-be-true opportunity."

Ross drummed his long fingers on the table, and an unreadable expression hovered behind his eyes. "I'm not like that. I never have jumped from one agent to another. I was going to stay with Harold and Smith until they double crossed me."

"I've heard the rumors about Harold and Smith, but I would like to hear the facts from you, if you don't mind," Charisma stated. "They are one of the top sports management companies. I have heard of athletes seeking them out."

The cracking sound of teeth grinding came from Ross's mouth, and his nostrils flaring showed Charisma that her potential client was trying not to lose his cool. "My agent, Baxter Harold, knew I wanted a tennis shoe commercial. I hinted about one from the first second he signed me. Six months into my contract, a huge sponsorship deal landed on his desk, and I heard about it."

Charisma waited while Ross rolled his shoulders to relieve the stress in his fit body. "Everyone else at the agency kept telling me I was going to get it, but I never heard from Baxter. Needless to say, I didn't land the deal, and I was pissed."

"What prevented you from landing the contract?"

"Baxter had a time limit of acceptance to get back with the shoe company, and he forgot to answer it."

"Did he tell you what made him forget?"

"He tried to give me this song and dance, but I wasn't having it. He lost me millions and a golden opportunity to land other contracts with the company."

"How long did it take for you to get a termination letter from him? I know he couldn't have giving you any trouble," Charisma retorted. "That incident was totally his fault."

"Oh, he tried to keep me until I told him that I was still in the time limit to leave him. After that, I got it from a courier, and I signed it the same day. I had never been so exultant in my life."

She had to make Ross believe that she wasn't going to play by those terms. Her job was very important to her, and her clients trust in her was highly important to her. "I'm sorry that happened to you, but I can assure you I tell my clients about ever offer that lands on my desk.

"In addition, I offer a confidentiality clause. The last thing I want is for you to be on television giving away any of my business secrets or what I charge you. On my side, you shouldn't be worried that I'll be telling your business in front of the press, either. I believe that the confidentiality clause helps you out more than it does me."

"I like what you said, and I can sense a good quality about you. How about we talk some more when we get back to the States? I'll get in touch with my lawyers, and we can see how things go from there?" Ross suggested, standing up.

Charisma wanted to leap up out of her seat, but she slowly stood up. "I think I can handle that. Do you still have the phone number to my job?"

"Yes, I think it's in my lawyer's rolodex. When will you be California?"

"Tomorrow night is my last night here," she answered.

"How about I'll give you a week to catch your breath, and I'll call you on the following Monday?"

"Fantastic," she smiled.

"Good. I was very impressed by what you had to tell me," Ross informed her coming around the table. "I'll give you my lawyer's fax number, and be sure to send him a contract so he can look over it before our meeting. I'm not saying I'm going to sign with you. This is just a 'getting to know you better' meeting."

"I understand completely."

Ross squeezed her shoulder and proceeded out the door without looking back at her, but that didn't matter. She had a second meeting with Ross. Lily never landed that back home. She was a step ahead of her rival.

Charisma glanced over at Dave and Keira's table, because she wanted to tell them her good news, but it was empty.

Where in the hell had the two of them gone?

Chapter Fourteen

"Keira, I don't know about this," Charisma complained, looking down at the violet dress her best friend had talked her into wearing. "I want to look sexy for Dave, but isn't this dress a little over the top?"

"You came in here less than an hour ago thinking I was somewhere with your man and demanded to know what the two of us were talking about over dinner," Keira snorted, walking around her, fixing the short hem of the nightgown that doubled as an appropriate dress in her best friend's eyes. "I thought you would be thrilled to know that Dave is waiting for you in his room."

"I'm glad he's there waiting for me, but I don't want to give him the wrong idea," Charisma exclaimed, slapping Keira's hand away from her leg. "Stop messing with that piece of thread."

"Sorry, but I only want you to look good since you won't be coming back here tonight," Keira defended, holding up her hands and taking two steps back.

"What makes you think I'm going to spend the night with Dave?"

"Honey, you're leaving in the morning to go back to California. Do you actually think that guy of yours isn't going to make your last night here out of this world?"

She shrugged one shoulder and picked up her bag off the night table. "I think you've been watching too many romance movies," Charisma told her on the way to the door.

"Don't worry. I put plenty of condoms in your purse," a voice filled with laughter taunted her as she went out the door, snapping it shut behind her.

"Wait until Keira finds a man. I'm going to torment her the same way she's doing me," Charisma groaned on the way to the elevator, ignoring the looks of an attractive bellboy who stopped and stared at her. She wasn't interested in a boy when she had a sexy-as-hell man waiting for her.

* * * *

Dave tossed back the last of his drink, placing the shot glass back down on the table. Charisma wasn't going to show up. She was probably out with Ross having a nightcap or something. Why would she want to be around him when a guy like Ross was interested in her? He was talking to Keira tonight, but he saw how the other man couldn't take his eyes off Charisma.

She was a stunning-looking woman and a man would be a complete idiot not to want her. This was his last night here on the island, and he wanted to spend it cementing his time with Charisma, but that wasn't going to happen now. She had stood him up.

Making his way over the mini bar, he was reaching for another bottle of bourbon when a knock at the door stopped him. "I told Brittney to carry her key. I don't know what I'm going to do with my sister," he said, moving away from the bar over to the door, swinging it open.

"Hello, handsome. I hope that I'm not too late," Charisma grinned at him wearing a sheer purple and lace nightie.

All the blood rushed from his head straight to his cock straining against the front of his jeans. *Shit.* How was it possible that the woman in front of him got hotter since the last time he laid eyes on her?

"I didn't think you were going to show up," he stated, leaning his shoulder against the doorjamb. Dave couldn't help spot how hard Charisma's nipples were through the smooth fabric.

"Do you know that you left your room only wearing a nightgown? I can see your perfect brown nipples outlined against the material." Dave ran one of his long fingers around the edge before tracing the top with his thumb.

Charisma shivered under his light stroke and he felt his ego go up another notch. No matter what he did, she constantly responded to him, "Is this for me or do you get this excited by any man's touch?" The question hovered in the air while he impatiently waited for an answer. He wasn't usually overly concerned with his past girlfriend's sexual history, but he wanted to be the only man that dominated Charisma's thoughts.

"Dave, you're the only man who makes my body leap to life like this," she responded, stepping closer to him, surrounding him with her body heat and unique scent. "How could you even think another man had this affect on me?"

A grin spread across his face like he was a child on Christmas morning after a visit from Santa, but that wasn't enough. He wanted proof of Charisma's attraction to him. "Show me."

Blinking a couple of times, Charisma face took on several expressions before she finally answered him. "Show you what?" The words tumbled from her mouth as she leaned back and stared up at him.

"How pretty your breasts are. I want to see them."

"I'll be more than happy to show them to you once we get inside your room," she promised, trying to move around him.

Blocking her entrance, he gave his head a small shake. "No, I want to see them now. It won't be the first time I've seen them. Come on, give me another peek at those beautiful perky treats."

Narrowing her eyes, Charisma shoved her purse under her arm. "I'm not exposing my breasts for you out here in the hallway. Anyone could pass by and see me." The heated look in her eyes almost made him back down, but he didn't. He would let Charisma only control so much, but when it came to foreplay and lovemaking, he like being the man.

"You're so damn hot. I know plenty of men that would give their right arm for a peek at you. However, this hallway is empty and if any man tried it while I was here, I'd kill him."

Silently, he waited in the open door of his hotel room for Charisma to make up her mind. He could see she was battling between her need to be in control and giving in to his request. She came off as so independent; however, he sensed a need in her.

It was buried deep, but he knew it was there. She wanted a strong man to take control for once in her life and give her the pleasure of being the one who got taken care of.

From talking with Jenisha, he had found out that Charisma was the one who dominated all of her past relationships, so it was time for her to be the spoiled one. He was more than eager to volunteer for the job, and it would be for a lifetime if she had enough courage to say yes.

"You're serious, aren't you?" her soft voice inquired. Moving her hand, the hallway light shined on the light purple fingernail polish as her slim fingers toyed with the straps of her dress.

His breath caught as she pulled it up and down several times. "Baby, when it comes to seeing your body, I'll never lie to you."

Skepticism passed over her face, and he silently cussed the men that made her doubt her self-worth. "What will I get if I show you mine?"

There was the woman that had stolen his heart all those months ago. Dave grinned at the returned spunk in his woman's voice. The way they bounced words back and forth was such a turn-on for him. It got him hotter, and his cock harder, in ways that Charisma could never dream of.

"I'll let you undress me," he responded, slipping his hands into the front pockets of his jeans. The actions caused the material to slip more, and Charisma got a sneak peak at his lower body.

She licked her lips as she ogled him. "You aren't wearing much as it is. How is that fair to me?" Charisma countered. Reaching out, she traced one of his nipples with her finger.

Giving Charisma's outfit another once over, his mouth kicked up into an inviting smile. *How was it possible for her to grow more inviting by the minute?* "I think we're wearing about the same amount of clothing. So, are you up to the challenge, Miss Miles?"

Dave searched from one end of the hallway down the other and he pinned Charisma with a questioning stare. He was beyond ready to live up to his end of the deal. The sight of this sex kitten taking off his clothes would keep his cock hard for days on end. Shit, he was about to spilt his jeans right this second.

"You don't think I'll do it?" she teased, stroking the top of her breasts with her fingers.

"Hey, I'm not saying a word. It's your choice, if you're up to the challenge." *Please let her do it.*

"It seems more like a Dave dare to me," she dared, playing with the straps of her dress again.

"I thought you looked like a woman that loved proving people wrong. I guess that I was wrong about you. You're all talk and no action," he countered, swallowing down a smile at the fire that leaped into Charisma's chocolate depths. She was about to give in. All he had to do was say the right words, and he would have everything he wanted.

Taking the tip of his fingers, he lightly ran it along the outside of Charisma's breasts. Her voice hitched in the middle of her throat as her chest almost fell out of the top of her dress from the deep breaths she was taking.

He was stunned by how ultra soft her body was tonight. Had she used a different lotion or body wash? There was something new about the texture of her skin. It was like he never experienced the perfection of her blemish-free skin until now.

"Charisma, please let me see you," the words were spoken in a low coaxing voice, hinting how much his tightly reigned control was slipping.

She swayed towards him as he removed his fingers from her sizzling body, and he lost what common sense he had left. No, tonight was for Charisma to prove how much she wanted to be with him.

"You've seen my breasts before," she mused. "Nothing has changed since the last time."

Tenderly, he cupped her chin in his hands and let his eyes flicker over her face. He was already in love with Charisma. She had come to mean everything to him in such a short period of time.

"I love you."

"NO!" she shouted, stepping back from him. "You don't know me well enough to say those words. We aren't like Hayward and True or Clinton and Jenisha. A love like theirs is a fairy-tale love, and only they're meant to have it.

"The two of us are sexual beings that love to flirt and have a good time with each other. Nothing more will ever come from this. I want to be with you tonight, and we when leave the island tomorrow, all of this will be a wonderful memory. You'll be back in Florida, and I have my life in California."

Angry that Charisma didn't believe in his love, Dave jerked her against his body. "Listen woman, I love you...no, damn it to hell. I'm in love with you. You're the woman I want to make love to every night and every morning for the rest of my life.

"Shit, I want to even introduce you to my crazy mother, and I never let any of my old girlfriends anywhere around her," he confessed, staring down into Charisma's astonished face. "I'm not going to let you run from me like you have everything else in your past. Yes, we might have to be involved in a long-distance relationship, but you're worth all the air travel in the world.

"Charisma, you aren't going to hide behind old fears when it comes to me. I'm a man that loves to get what he wants and without a doubt in my mind, I want you in my life. We don't need what our friends have, because we aren't them. We're going to make our own fairy-tale ending. But it won't work unless you're willing to give me a chance...*fuck*, give us a chance," Dave shouted, terrified that he wasn't getting through to her. "Can you do that?"

"You're hurting my arms."

Instantly, he let her go and stepped back, running his hands over his short, spiky hair. "I'm sorry."

Closing his eyes, he started to count backwards from ten hoping it would calm his nerves. He must be out of his mind to say those things to Charisma when she hadn't admitted to feeling anything more than an attraction to him.

"Dave, look at me," Charisma said.

"What is it?" Dave asked, opening his eyes, and he almost fell back into the room when he saw the incredible sight in front of him. "You're so fucking perfect."

Charisma's nightgown that was doubling as a dress tonight was around her womanly hips exposing her mouth-watering breasts. He cupped their fullness in his hands before dropping his head and sucking one pebble-hard nipple into his mouth.

Chapter Fifteen

Charisma moaned deep as Dave wrapped his arms around her body and carried her into his hotel room. Kicking the door closed with the heel of his shoe, his tongue caressed her sensitive swollen nipples as he laid her gently on the bed.

"I didn't think you would do it," he whispered, lifting his head from her breasts.

"I wasn't about to back down from your challenge," she answered, running the tips of her fingers over his swollen lips. "Besides, I've been fantasizing about this since the first time you kissed me."

She couldn't get over how perfect it felt to be here like this with Dave. He had dug deep and found the part of her that guys in her past never wanted to find. Her shell hadn't scared him off. If anything, it seemed to turn him on even more. What if this turned out to be more than just a pleasure trip? She wasn't ready to let Dave take up a huge part of her life, not when she had so many problems going on back home.

"What has put that expression on your beautiful face?" Dave inquired, staring into her eyes while he slipped the dress off her body. It was thrown across the room before she could say a word.

The sensations that shot heat through her limbs made her quiver. She made a noise as Dave captured her mouth again with his before she could answer. His mouth was devouring hers and there wasn't a thing she wanted to do about it. He touched her again, trailing his hands down her breasts, over her stomach, slipping her panties from her body, dropping them to the floor.

This time her body responded more intimately to his like they were old lovers coming back together. Charisma wrapped her arms around Dave pulling his closer to her body. She answered the pressure of his kisses with a headlong response, something she couldn't hide.

Lifting his mouth from hers, Dave's eyes searched her face. "You're exquisite," he said, his voice rough with arousal turning her body on even more. "You've got to be the most perfect woman God has ever created."

Standing up, Dave stripped the remainder of his clothes from his body. Charisma watched him through a daze of burning desire. He looked down at her, his body powerful and tense with its damp, bronzed muscles and with the flames tattoo that circled his navel leading down to his powerful erection.

"I want this night to make you a part of me forever," Dave whispered enigmatically, sliding his body back on top of hers. He played with her mouth, sending tiny shock throughout her.

Charisma tore her mouth away trying to capture her breath. "Dave, don't tease me like this," She wept. "Dave, please do something."

She moved against his body, whimpering. It took everything in his power to hold back, but he did. "You have to want more than sex," he exclaimed, breathing softly against her mouth. "I want this to be something deeper."

"I do…!"

"I don't feel that you do." Dave touched her breasts, stroking the sensitive nipples slowly, driving her crazy. His mouth was the devil, taunting, teasing, arousing, insistent, and her body was his playground.

All the while, she moaned, and her body writhed around on the bed praying Dave would end her aching. "I

MARIE ROCHELLE

can't stand it any longer," she sobbed, scratching at his muscular back.

"Baby, neither can I," he confessed against her damp neck. Dave moved slowly connecting their bodies for the first time, and Charisma almost screamed from the pleasure of it.

She tried to move, but Dave grabbed her hips. He was above her watching her with dark eyes that burned with fervor. "Don't move. Lie still. I don't want to hurt you. Give your body a chance to get used to mine. You're so damn tight. Has it been a while for you?"

"Yes...." Charisma confessed, squirming around on the bed trying to get used to the thickness of Dave's cock inside of her. "Is that a problem?

"Hell no," he groaned then pushed down. "Am I hurting you? That is the last thing that I'd ever want to do."

The blatant concern in his deep voice almost brought tears to her eyes. Not one of the guys in her past sexual experiences ever cared enough to ask her. She could sense that Dave was holding back until she got her pleasure first, and she couldn't let him do it. She wanted them to explode together.

"No, you aren't hurting me."

Spreading her legs wider, she let Dave's body press against her more intimately. She never felt anything like this before. It was like he was supposed to here like this with her. Charisma trembled with the awe of it as she stroked his shoulders and ran her hands down his back.

"Charisma," he whispered. "If you keep doing that, I'm going to lose control," Dave shuddered dropping his head down into her shoulder.

"Lose control," Charisma encouraged, scratching at his back. "I want to remember this night for the rest of my life."

She closed her eyes as Dave kissed the side of her neck, moving around until his talented mouth reconnected with hers. Slipping her arms around his neck, Charisma sucked in a deep breath as Dave began to move. Waves of pleasure started tingling throughout her body as the pace sped up.

Somewhere during the second round of tiny shock waves of bliss, her eyes opened, and she looked at Dave. She had never thought about looking until now, and it was nothing like she had ever experienced before. Dave's face was taunted with desire, and it was like he sensed her gaze, because his eyes flew open trapping her with their dark magic.

"Shit," he breathed, reaching down to wrap her legs around his hips. "You're burning me up. I can't hold back any longer. Baby, please help me hold back."

"No, join me. I want us to be together," she murmured, nibbling at his full bottom lip with her teeth.

The pleasure was nearing. She could feel it sneaking up on her body in little doses, but it was scaring her. She felt like she was losing a part of herself tonight to this man she had fought so hard to keep away. "Dave?" she cried, feeling like her control was slipping.

"Baby, let it come. Let me watch you. I want to see the pleasure in your eyes when I make you come for the very first time." He grabbed her wrists and gently pinned them against the bed and pushed down one last time.

Dave's face blurred in front of hers as the rush hit over and over until she felt like she was floating above her body. Somewhere in the back of her mind, Charisma heard Dave's shouting his release, but she couldn't speak. Her body was still coming back down to earth. Minutes later, fear set in as she realized that she had never experience anything like that in her life.

"That was unbelievable," Dave groaned, kissing her breasts, moving his way back up to her mouth. "I never thought I would find that kind of completeness with a woman." He gently separated their bodies, rolled to the side, and held her against his chest.

"I know this is new for you, but I swear I won't be like those jerks in your past. I want us to have a future together."

"You keep saying that," Charisma whispered, stroking the skin above Dave's left nipple. What in the hell was she going to do? Was she really ready to have a permanent relationship at this time in her life?

Growling, Dave placed his hand on the top of hers. "You shouldn't do that. It won't take much to get my cock hard for you again, and I don't think your body is ready. We were going at it for a while, and you've to be a little sore."

"I'm used to having sex with a guy more than once in a night."

"We made love," Dave corrected, giving her a little squeeze, "and I'm pretty sure that you haven't slept with a lot of guys in your past that are built like me. Am I right?"

"You're right," she admitted. Lord, Dave was a house compared to her past three boyfriends.

"How about we take a quick nap and then try in a few hours?" he suggested, covering their damp bodies. "I want you to get use to me in small doses, because in the near future I want to spend the whole day making love to this luscious body of yours."

"Okay," Charisma agreed softly. She didn't have the heart to tell Dave that when he woke up she wouldn't be in his bed or, for that fact, Jamaica.

Chapter Sixteen

Los Angles, California, two weeks later

"I can't *believe* you just had sex with him and left him in bed asleep," Keira complained taking a sip of her coffee. "Has he tried getting in touch with you?"

The noise around the café blocked out their conversation for people sitting at a nearby table, and Charisma was glad about that. She didn't want everyone in the world knowing about her business or what craziness happened on her trip to Jamaica. Shit, she had got so caught up in the moment that Dave hadn't even used a condom.

"Yes, he had left several messages on my answering machine, and I only returned one call telling him I wasn't pregnant," Charisma exclaimed. "Lord, I can't even face Jenisha. I wasn't about to tell her what transpired on my vacation. But of course, Dave had to confide in Clinton."

"Which means Jenisha called you the second she found out about your sexy adventure?" Keira teased.

"She thinks Dave and I are an item now."

"Aren't you?"

"No," Charisma shouted then lowered her voice when Keira gave her a look. "Dave makes me feel things that I don't want to feel. I've to work on saving my job from Lily. We both know she's 'using her assets' to steal my job away from me."

"Why don't you go and complain to your boss?"

"Who do you think she was sleeping with first?" Charisma groaned, already hating that she was back at work. Jamaica had relaxed her so much. Who knew that Dave could move his big body like that? It killed her to sneak out of that bed after he had fallen to sleep, but if she stayed a moment later…it wouldn't have been good.

"You're thinking about him, aren't you?" Keira inquired, drumming her fingers on the tabletop.

"About who?" Charisma hedged.

"Dave."

"No. I told you there isn't anything between the two of us."

"So, it was just sex and you wouldn't care if he's already moved on to the next woman?"

Her stomach hurt at the thought of Dave loving someone else like he did her. Surely, he couldn't jump into another woman's bed so easily? "I don't care if he does," she shrugged.

"Okay. I'll let you win this round, but I'm waiting until I get to tell you 'I told you so'," Keira answered waving for the check.

"That day is never going to happen," Charisma mumbled under her breath, wishing her friend would leave it alone.

"Yes, it will. Just remember I look good in red."

"Why are you telling me what color you look good in?" Charisma frowned.

"I want you to know in ahead of time for when you pick out my maid of honor dress. I can't be wearing a color that doesn't look amazing on me."

"I'm not about to marry Dave Turner," she hissed. "I'm not made for the fairy tale life like True and Jenisha."

"I'll be sure to remind you of this conversation when you're getting ready for your wedding."

Charisma hated that Keira loved teasing her. Sometimes it would drive her up one wall and right down another one. "Keep it up, and I swear I'm not going to let you hear the last of it when you fall in love."

"Did you admit that you're in love with muscles?" Keira grinned.

"Nope...I never said a word about being in love with anyone," Charisma said getting up from the table. "Now, I've to get back to work. Knowing that bitch Lily, she has already moved me out of my office."

Standing up, Keira placed some money down on the table for the waiter. "Let me walk you back to your car. I'm not done teasing you."

"You're such a good friend," she moaned, heading for the door.

"I know I am," Keira agreed, following her out.

* * * *

"I can't believe she just left without saying goodbye. I thought we shared something, but I guess I was wrong." Dave accepted the cup of coffee True gave him, wrapping his hands around the warm mug.

"Charisma is a very hard woman to read. She loves her independence, but I know that you can win her over," Hayward replied, handing his empty mug to his wife. "Look, I won True over the first day she saw me."

"Keep it up, and you'll be sleeping on the couch tonight," True teased, trying to slip past her husband into the other room.

"You know that I love you," Hayward said slipping him arms around her as much as her pregnant stomach would allow.

"Mr. Campbell, you better love me. We're about to have four kids under the age of five," True sighed, wiggling away from Hayward and went into the other room.

Dave saw how Hayward's eyes never left his wife until she was sitting down on the couch with her feet evaluated. "I can't believe you're having twins again."

"Yeah and boys at that," Hayward grinned, looking back at him. "I'm very excited and so is True, but she has been more tired lately. I think taking care of the boys while I'm at work is getting to her. I might stop traveling back and forth now. Clinton is doing a good job at handling both offices so far."

"I envy the both of you," he confessed. "You and Clinton are with the women you love having kids, and the woman I want is running from me."

"Did you forget how I almost lost True and my boys because I lied to her?" Hayward whispered, glancing at his wife trying not to fall asleep on the couch. "How about when Clinton married Jenisha and then almost lost her? We both had a hard time getting the women we loved to marry us."

"Charisma is totally different from True and Jenisha. She's so controlled in everything she does. She stays so focused like nothing around her can get in and break her concentration," Dave complained, remembering how hard it was to get Charisma to even date him while they were in Jamaica.

"She does have a strong personality. I noticed that the few times I've meet her, but it doesn't show when she's with Kevin and Evan. She's really good with the boys. They love their Aunt Charisma."

Dave took a long swallow of his coffee before placing it back on the table. "Tell me how to win her over. I'm so in love with her, but she's hiding from me. I've called her numerous times and she only called back once to tell me she wasn't pregnant."

"Did you want her to be pregnant?"

"Yes, I did. However, I didn't want that as the solution to getting her to come back to me."

"Let me be honest with you. From what I've heard, Charisma doesn't believe in a long-term commitment. She's more like the love them and leave them type. Don't get me wrong. I like her, but I don't want her hurting you."

"I'm not going to get hurt by Charisma. I know she's the one for me. Did you give up on True when she went away, and you couldn't find her for months? Wasn't she worth waiting for?"

"I would have waited for True for as long as she needed, because I was the one who had lied to her," Hayward answered, getting up from the table. "You aren't lying to Charisma, so she shouldn't be playing games with you."

Dave took another long gulp of his coffee and almost choked on the taste of it. He couldn't tell Hayward about Trish. She wasn't a part of his life now. He had broken things off with her the second he got back from his trip. His heart had swelled with a feeling he had never felt before when he spotted Charisma on that beach.

"Dave, you aren't lying to Charisma, are you?" Hayward questioned, rejoining him at the table. "You've seen first hand what lying will get you."

"No. I'm not doing anything of the sort to Charisma." *The less Hayward knew, the better off he would be,* Dave thought.

"I hope you're telling me the truth, because Charisma doesn't look like she would be forgiving as True or Jenisha."

"I am." Pushing his chair away from the table, Dave stood and grabbed his light jacket off the back. "Thanks for letting me crash here. I didn't want to be at home, and Brittney is gone to cheerleading camp. She wasn't home twenty-four hours before she was right back out the door."

"How is Brittney?" Hayward asked as he walked Dave to the front door past a sleeping True.

"She's a typical teenager," he grinned. "I try to keep her in line, but sometimes I know she gets away with murder."

"What does she think about Charisma? With their personalities, I would think that the two of them would always be at each other throats."

Dave didn't even want to think about what would happen when Brittney and Charisma met for the first time. Two strong-willed females under one roof won't be a good thing.

"They haven't met yet," Dave answered, opening the door. "I'm just praying when they do, Brittney will be on her best behavior, and Charisma won't be in one of her moods."

"I'm sure when Brittney realizes how much Charisma means to you, she'll be on her best behavior," Hayward answered, following him out of the porch.

"I hope your right, because I love Charisma and she's going to be a part of my life."

"Well, if you need a place to come again, you're more than welcome to come back. Kevin and Evan should be home then. You know they'll look for a new tattoo."

"Yeah, they loved the fake ones that I brought them last time," Dave laughed on the way to his car. "How long did they stay on?"

"For almost two weeks, and they loved it," Hayward chuckled, waving at him as he got into the rental car.

"Tell True goodbye, and I'll call you later on in the week." Dave waved goodbye as he pulled out of the driveway and headed for the airport. All the way to his destination, he couldn't stop thinking about how wonderful it had felt in Jamaica when he went to sleep with Charisma in his arms. It was like time had stopped and everything he had ever wanted was there with him.

"How can I get her to understand that we are meant to be together? What else do I have to do for her to see me and not be scared of her emotions," he muttered aloud.

Dave knew one thing for sure. Charisma was going to stop hiding from him because after the night they shared, she was his, and he wasn't about to let her go for anything.

Chapter Seventeen

"It must be fun to be able to take off any time you want to and go on an island vacation," Lily taunted as she swayed into her office. "The rest of us was here working hard to land new clients while you were out having fun in the sun. I don't think that looks good to the boss, do you?"

Slinging her pen down on the table in front of the couch, Charisma got up from the seat and made her way back over to her desk. She couldn't believe Lily just barged in like she already owned it. This was still her personal space until someone told her different.

"Lily, why are you here? I'm busy, and I don't have any extra time to deal with you at the moment. Besides, there aren't any men in here for you to kiss up to."

"Jealousy doesn't look good on you, Charisma. I can't help that you don't have a man." Smirking, Lily crossed her arms over her breasts and gave her a smug look. The kind of look that made a person fight the urge to slap the taste out of someone's mouth.

"I believe you're wrong. Charisma does have a man," a rich voice replied from the open doorway.

Charisma's eyes flew over to the door and widened at the shock of seeing Dave standing there looking too gorgeous in a black suit with an azure shirt unbuttoned at the neck. Just the sight of him made her wet, as the last time they were together came rushing back to her in a flash.

"Dave, what are you doing here?" Charisma asked. She didn't miss how Lily licked her lips as her eyes traveled over Dave's perfect body displayed beautifully in the suit. She didn't know he even owned something like that. She was so used to seeing him in shorts and a T-shirt. The new look really looked good on him.

"I came to see my girlfriend," he whispered, meeting her halfway. "Are you surprised?"

"You know that I am," she exclaimed, staring up at him. Lord, how was it possible for this man to get better looking than he already was? "How long are you going to be in town?"

"Can I get a kiss?" Dave asked, totally throwing her off.

"Hmmm, I have someone in the office." Charisma wasn't about to give Lily a free show of Dave for any reason.

"I don't care. I want a kiss." Strong arms wrapped around her waist and yanked her fully against his chest. Before she knew what happening, Dave's mouth was on hers.

His mouth was moist, firm, and demanded a response from her. Parting her lips, Charisma raised herself to meet his kiss. All thoughts of Lily, along with anyone else, left her mind the second Dave's masterful tongue entered her mouth. Moaning, she pressed her body fully to his, wanting to draw out this pleasure as much as she could. It had been such a long time since she had been kissed like this.

Leaving her mouth burning with fire and unspoken promises, Dave nibbled at the side of her neck and ran his hands down her back. Cupping her butt, he pressed her against his rising cock. "Baby, I want you so much," the words brushed over her skin softly and sinfully.

"Sorry to interrupt, but did the two of you forget that I was here?" Lily's shrewd voice cut in, breaking them slowly apart.

"Sorry about that," Dave apologized, running his thumb over her bottom lip. "I just have missed you so much. I couldn't resist."

Touching his hand, Charisma moved it away from her mouth before it made her do something she shouldn't. "That's okay. I didn't mind at all," she grinned and directed her attention back to Lily. "Do you mind leaving? I'm sure whatever you had to tell me can wait now."

Lily glared at her for a few minutes before she gave Dave another once over and sauntered from the room swinging her non-existent hips. Charisma flinched as the door slammed shut behind her rival.

"I can't stand that bitch. I wish the ground would open up and swallow her skinny ass," she muttered, moving away from Dave.

"Now, don't let her get to you. Don't you know she's just jealous that you're everything she wants to be, but she'll never achieve it?"

"I need you around all the time," Charisma grinned. Spinning around she tried not to envision how good Dave looked naked a few weeks ago. She couldn't let herself fall for the guy. He had the ability to take her places that no other man had. "You're very good at stroking the ego."

"If you stop running from me all the time, I'll show you what else I'm good at, too," Dave retorted. "I haven't forgotten about that certain spot on your body that likes to be licked. How many times did you come when I did that?"

Gasping, Charisma pressed her hand to her chest and fell back against her desk. *Damn it!* Why did he have to go there? She was doing pretty well until he brought that shit up. He was the first man that ever found that *spot* on her body.

"Hmmm, what are you doing here? Do we need to talk about something?" she asked, purposely avoiding going down the wrong path with Dave.

"Us." The answer was short and to the point.

Frowning, Charisma sat down on the desk and waved towards the empty seat in front of her. "Us? I'm not following you."

Taking a seat, Dave leaned forward and traced the side of her leg with one long finger. "You know what I'm talking about. I woke up the next morning in Jamaica, and you were gone. Why didn't you tell me you were leaving so early? We could have flown home together. I wanted to introduce you to my sister."

"You looked so sexy asleep, and I didn't want to wake you. Keira and I decided to catch an early flight at the last minute," she lied, brushing Dave's nerve-tingling finger off her leg, but he placed it back, slipping it between her thighs instead.

"The bed smelled like you, sweet and sinful. When I woke, I was hard, alone, and cold," he whispered, easing another finger between her thighs. "For a second, I thought you might be in the shower. I jumped out of the bed to join you, only to be disappointed."

"I'm sorry that I got your hopes up," Charisma answered, squirming on the desk as Dave's fingers got closer to her underwear. She could feel her panties getting soaked at the thought of him touching her.

"I think you need to do something about it," he growled, pushing her skirt up past her hips.

"What are you doing?" Charisma hissed, reaching for her mini-skirt.

"Don't do that," he ordered, slapping her hands away. "I want to see what kind of underwear you're wearing. Do you know that a man can tell a lot about a woman from her panties?" Dave mused, eyeing her pink thong.

Keep your mouth shut. That thought lasted for about one second before she asked. "What does mine say about me?"

The corners of Dave's mouth kicked up into a sexy grin as he traced the edges of her underwear with his index finger. "Why should I tell you anything? You've been so mean to me. I had such a wonderful last day planned for us in Jamaica, and I wasn't able to do any of it because of you."

"Will saying I'm sorry make it better?" Charisma asked, smiling.

"No, you aren't going to charm me," Dave grinned as he continued to torture her with his fingers. "I should make you pay for leaving me rock hard and alone."

"Ohhh…I don't know if you're man enough to do this. I think I'm pretty strong," she teased back, trying to block out the building orgasms working its way into her body. *Shit…Dave's fingers needed to be outlawed*, she thought.

"Even better, because what man doesn't love a strong, independent woman?' he answered, tugging her underwear down her legs dropping them on the floor.

"Hey, you can't do that," Charisma hissed. "What if someone walks in?" She was enjoying their fun and games, but she wasn't going to lose her job because of it. Lily was looking for anything to get her fired.

"Shh…no one is going to come in," Dave whispered, pushing her down on the desk covering her body with his.

Her heart sped up at the look in Dave's eyes. She wasn't ready to recognize what it was yet. It was way too soon in their relationship to be thinking about that. She was going to live in the moment with Dave and not get emotionally attached to him. He wasn't going to stay around for the long haul, either.

"What put that frown on your face?" Dave asked, kissing her forehead. "Can't have you getting wrinkles on this gorgeous face of yours."

"Would you still want to date me if I got wrinkles?"

"I want to do more than date you, but you aren't ready to hear that yet. So yes, I'll want to date you with wrinkles," he confessed, kissing the side of her neck, placing his hands by her head.

Charisma wanted to believe Dave so badly, but past experiences was making her nervous of giving in totally to the man above her. "I thought you wanted to finish what we had in Jamaica. It seems like we're doing a lot of talking to me," she replied, running her hands over Dave's spiky hair.

"Are you really ready to live that dangerous?" he asked, working on the buttons on her blouse. "Once I start making love to you, I'm not going to be able to stop. The door isn't locked, and anyone could walk in. I like a little danger in my life, do you?" Dave moved her shirt away from her breasts and ran his thumb over her nipples.

"I sure am," she moaned, pressing her breast deeper into his palm. Charisma shoved any of rational thoughts to the back of her mind as Dave's fingertips played with her. She had never let go like this in the past. What was causing her to do so now?

"Beauty, you're so perfect. What have I done to deserve you?" Just as Dave moved his head towards her swollen nipples and give her what she wanted, the sound of Wyclef broke into their paradise.

Jumping, Charisma pushed Dave off her body. "What in the hell is that noise?" she snapped, looking at his body.

Grinning, Dave stepped back from her and pulled a cell phone from his slacks. "Sorry, it's my phone. Don't go anywhere. Let me deal with this, and we can get back to what we were doing." Winking at her, Dave moved over to her window and took the call.

Reality set in as the coolness of the room hit her chest making her already swollen nipples harder. Charisma closed her blouse and slipped off the desk. She took a quick peek at Dave before she made a beeline for her private bathroom. Once she got inside, she locked the door and glanced at herself in the mirror.

The woman staring back at her was unrecognizable. Her lips were swollen from all of kisses Dave kept planting on her. Despite the fact her hair was cut short, it was sticking out all over her head making it look like she had spent the afternoon making love. Shaking her head, Charisma quickly fixed her clothes and her hair. She knew that she couldn't let Dave seduce her like that again. When it came to him, she had no willpower. One look from those dark pool of chocolate eyes and she was a goner.

"Girl…you've to stay away from him. If he asks you out on another date, turn him down. Dave Turner is the man you have been trying to avoid most of your life. He sees the part of you that you want to keep hidden."

She hated to do him like that because Dave was a good guy, but she wasn't ready for someone like him in her life. She was way too independent and self-sufficient to let a man control her heart and soul. It was best to end things with Dave before they went any further, and she wouldn't want to let him go.

"Okay, just go out there and tell him you aren't interested in a relationship just based on good sex…hell, incredible sex," she scolded herself before opening the bathroom door.

Standing in the middle of her office, Charisma straightened her clothes and tried to get her mind back on her job. Pausing by her desk, she looked for her underwear. They were gone and so was Dave.

"Wait until I see him. I'm going to kill him. I can't go all day without wearing any underwear," she complained, slipping behind her desk. Logging onto her computer, Charisma started checking her emails and was halfway through them when her office door opened, and her boss walked through.

"Mr. Thurman, can I help you?" she asked, wondering what in the hell he wanted with her. She was in no mood to deal with her boss after dealing with Dave and Lily in the same day.

"I heard that you had a run-in with Lily. I'm coming to see if were you okay," her boss inquired, taking a seat despite the fact she didn't offer one.

"I'm fine and Miss Kane and I didn't have a run-in. I had a visitor, and I asked her politely to leave."

"Are you sure that's all that happen?" Mr. Thurman drilled her. Then she felt something brushing against her inside of her leg.

Charisma swatted her thigh and touched something hard and warm. Sliding her chair back, she barely held her gasp of surprise at the sight of Dave under her desk. How in the hell did he get his big-ass body under there? What was he up to now? She hated to think about it, but there was no way she would let Mr. Thurman know Dave was under there. Scooting her seat closer to her desk, Charisma rested her elbows on the top, "Yes, I'm positive that is all. Lily got upset and stormed out of the room, but I wouldn't call that a fight."

She tried to stay still as two strong hands spread her legs as wide as they would go inside her seat. She couldn't react because her boss would come over and check to see what was the matter with her.

"Charisma, I know that you and Lily aren't getting along since you're both fighting for the same job, but I don't think you should be rude to her."

"I wasn't..." Her voice trailed off as Dave slipped two thick fingers inside of her, making her come almost instantly. Charisma blew out a breath and tried to calm down, but it wasn't working. She dropped one of her hands underneath the desk and tried to shove him back, but that only made him add another finger.

"Charisma, are you okay?" Mr. Thurman asked with a slight frown to his face. "You don't look too good."

Biting her lip, she swallowed down a moan and tried to gain back some of her control. "I'm fine. It just has been a long day," she lied, silently cursing the man beneath her desk.

"Are you sure? You're breathing pretty hard. Do you need a drink of water?"

"No, sir. I'm fine," she hissed, squirming around in the chair as Dave's fingers were replaced by his tongue. Charisma would have completely leaped in the air if he hadn't tightened his grip on her thighs.

"Oh my God," she groaned, digging her nails into the arms of the chair. Dave eased his hand under her butt pressing her wetness closer to his mouth. It would only be a matter of time before she exploded.

"Charisma, I'm getting concerned about you. You really don't look good. Are you positive that you're alright?" Mr. Thurman asked as he started to stand up.

SHIT! She couldn't let him come over here and find Dave. It would be the end of her career. Charisma slowly took several deep breaths trying to focus on her boss and not the tongue lapping at her juices.

"Honestly, I'm fine. Mr. Thurman. Please don't get up," she said, loosening her grip on the chair. "I didn't sleep well last night, and I went to bed without eating," she lied, blocking out Dave's mouth that had moved. Now he was nibbling at the inside of her thighs.

"I'm certain after I get something inside of me, I'll be back to my old self." *HOLY SHIT!!!* Charisma's mind screamed as Dave thrust two long fingers deep inside her body making her orgasms erupted. She didn't have time to regain her senses before he was licking her clean.

Her boss eyed her a few seconds before he stood up. "Charisma, why don't you take an early lunch? You don't look good at all. I don't need you passing out at work."

Slipping her hand underneath her desk, Charisma held Dave's head against her enjoying the lingering sensations of her orgasm. "I have a lunch date. Do you mind if I took a two hour lunch? I can make up the time later on in the week."

Mr. Thurman paused at the door and looked back at her over his shoulder. "No, take the longer lunch. You can write it off as a business lunch," he exclaimed then went out the door, closing it behind him.

Charisma waited a few minutes to make sure her boss was gone before she shoved her chair back and glared down into Dave's smiling face. "What in the hell did you do that for?" she demanded, wishing her body didn't want a repeat performance.

Pushing her chair completely out of the way, Dave got from under her desk and stood up to his full height. "You were so tense. I thought you needed to relax. Did it help you?" An irresistibly devastating grin tugged at the side of his mouth, highlighting the dark richness of Dave's eyes.

"You know that it did, darn you. But I almost died when my boss asked me what was wrong."

"I thought you did a good job of staying calm." Dave stepped closer to her and pulled her out of the chair, tugging her to his body.

The touch of Dave's erection brushing against her stomach made her eyes dart up to his. "It feels like you need to release a little tension of your own," she whispered, slipping her hand between their bodies. *What happened to her breaking off with Dave?* her mind thought as she cupped his cock in her hand.

His cock jerked at her light touch. "Beauty, don't do that. You've a lunch date. We can't get into this," Dave growled, resting his forehead against hers.

"I lied."

"Lied about what?" Dave asked, placing his hands on top her hands brushing his erection against her palm.

"I lied about having a lunch date. I thought maybe you might want to finish what we started here in this room. I can feel that you're more than capable."

Dave titled her head back with his free hand. He searched her face like he was looking for a hidden secret. When he finally spoke, his voice was low and tender, almost like a murmur. "Sweetheart, that was for you, not me. I'll be okay. Why don't you take that lunch and spend it with Keira. I'm in town to visit an old friend anyway."

"Do I know this old friend?" she hedged, removing her hand from underneath his.

"I don't think that you do."

"Are you going to tell me who it is?"

Laughing, Dave kissed the side of her neck. "It's someone who I used to work with."

"Does this person have a name?" she inquired, not liking how Dave was stringing her along. "Or do you not want me to know?" Charisma hated her jealousy but she couldn't help it.

"Jim Russell," he answered with a smug look like he knew she was jealous, but he didn't say a word.

A smile lit up her face. "Oh, I know him. He's cute. I like the long-hair thing," Charisma responded, moving away from a stunned Dave. "Have fun, and tell him I said hi."

A hand settled on her shoulder and spun her back around. "How do you know him?"

She couldn't ignore the heated look in Dave's eyes or the possessiveness of his tone. He thought that she and Jim were more than acquaintances. "Calm down, big boy. Jenisha introduced me to him one time at Bryant. I think you were gone to get supplies with Clinton. Nice guy, but he seemed a little lost."

Dave's attitude instantly changed after she explained her connection to his former co-worker. "Back then, he was going through a bad divorce, and now his wife won't let him see his little boy."

"Thanks so sad. How old is he?"

"I think Trevor turned six the other day, and Jim wasn't allowed to come to the party," Dave sighed shaking his head. "He dropped off the present and left. Kathy let Jim spend time with him the other day."

"God, that had to be hard on him. I know how much Clinton misses the kids when Jenisha brings them for a visit. However, Hayward is worse than him."

Dave chuckled. "Hayward is bad when it comes to True. I went for a visit, and she couldn't leave his sight. I think he's driving her up the wall, but you can see how much he loves her and their kids."

Charisma started to feel a little uneasy with the way the conversation was turning. Dave hadn't kept his feelings a secret about her, but she wasn't the type of woman he needed in his life.

"I agree. True and Jenisha lucked out when it came to good husbands," she answered, moving away from Dave. "I don't want to keep you since Jim is waiting. But if I was you, I might freshen up before I go see him."

Opening her top desk drawer, she pulled out her purse and slipped past him. "You're more than welcome to use my bathroom. There's an extra toothbrush and mouthwash in the cabinet above the sink."

Charisma was halfway at the door when she heard, "I'll let you go this time, but you can't keep running from your future. We're going to talk, and it will be sooner than later."

Opening the door, she ran out without looking back. She knew without a doubt that Dave was looking at her, and she wasn't ready to see what was in his eyes. Dave wasn't her future, and the quicker he understood that, the better his life would be.

Chapter Eighteen

"Hey old man, I thought you had stood me up," Dave laughed as he stood up and hugged his former co-worker Jim Russell. He sat back down and waited to hear what held up his friend. He wouldn't put it past his buddy's ex-wife to be involved.

"No, I had to take Trevor back to Kathy and listen to another one of her lectures," Jim replied as he sat down at the table covered with a checkered tablecloth and matching napkins.

"What was her problem this time?" Dave groaned, knowing the way Kathy still picked at Jim for no reason. The sad thing was he thought that Jim was still in love with his ex.

"Kathy wanted more money, and I didn't have any extra money to give her. You remember the last time we talked, I told you I was saving up for my own shop?"

"Sure…did you find a shop outside of town that you were interested in?" Dave asked. "I remember that you said you had talked to the owner a couple of times about it. Have you heard back from him yet?"

Jim shook his head causing his ponytail to swing in the back. "No. I'm supposed to meet with him again at the middle of the month and get another tour, but the place is perfect! He's even going to include his bikes, because he has a daughter and she doesn't have any interest in the business."

"Man…that's wonderful. I wish you the best of luck," Dave replied, wishing he was having better luck with his job efforts. But the new CCD building in Florida wasn't ready to open yet. He needed to talk with Clinton about that while he was in town.

"Hey, I haven't talked to you in a while. How are things with you? Dating any sexy women? I know you don't stay single long," Jim joked reclining back in his seat.

"I'm dating a sexy woman, but she is playing very hard to get, and it's driving me up the wall," he growled as an image of Charisma flashed in his mind. All beauty and spunk smiled back at him, but he still sensed a small part of Charisma that she was keeping hidden from him.

"I bet I know who it is." Jim stated, sitting up. "There's only one woman that you've been rock hard for since the day you laid eyes on her."

"And who would that be?"

"Charisma Miles, and I've to agree she is one beautiful woman. So what would she want with your ugly mug?"

"Charisma and I have come a long way since I last talked about her. But it isn't going as fast as I want it, and by the way, stop referring to my woman's looks. Isn't it about time you found someone for yourself anyway?"

"Fuck no!" Jim shouted and quickly lowered his voice. "I've had enough with the opposite sex for a while. If I do get with another woman, it will be only to scratch an itch and nothing else."

Dave wasn't surprised by his friend's cruel response and he understood it, but he wished Jim would change his mind. "Come on…don't let Kathy win. I'm sure there has to be a woman out there dumb enough to fall in love with you."

"See? You've fallen in love and now you're all weak. That happened to me once, and that was enough for me."

"Charisma hasn't made me weak at all. Honestly, she has made me see the man I want to become. She has dated so many losers in the past that she's afraid to give me a chance."

"God," Jim groaned, but a small smile teased his lips. "You're sounding more like Hayward and Clinton. I remember how they were when they fell in love."

"You don't know what you're missing. There's nothing like a good woman in your life. You wait and see," Dave insisted.

"You'll be waiting for a lifetime, but I'm not falling in love again. I'm just going to work and take care of Trevor."

"I don't see the great Jim Russell without a woman in his life. Weren't you the one that had a date every night until you married your ex-wife?"

"That was when I was younger."

"You aren't old now," Dave answered, wondering how to get his friend out of this mindset. He hated that Kathy had made Jim like this.

"Tell that to Kathy. Or didn't you know that she divorced me for a boy that was twenty-one?" Jim asked with more than a little hurt in his voice. "I came home and caught the two of them in my bed."

Dave had heard the rumors, but he still couldn't believe it was true. He thought Kathy was a bitch the first time he met her, but he kept it to himself.

"You never liked Kathy, did you?" Jim asked. "She told me that you always gave her this look."

He wasn't about to tell Jim about the time Kathy came on to him at the birthday barbeque two years ago. Jim was like a big brother to him, and he wasn't going to end their friendship over something stupid.

"Clinton told me about what happened at the birthday party."

"I don't know what you're talking about," Dave lied.

"Clinton saw Kathy kiss you and how quickly you pushed her away. Why didn't you tell me?"

Dave arched an eyebrow. "Would you have believed me back then?"

"No, I wouldn't have," Jim confessed. "I was totally blinded by love for Kathy."

"See? That's why I kept it to myself." He wasn't about to lose another friend. The loss of Jackson had almost killed him.

"Hey, man," Jim said, making him come back from the past. "Jackson's death wasn't your fault. You have to know that."

"You can say that all you want, but I was the one that got him started lifting weights in the first place," Dave exclaimed. "He might still be alive if I'd just left him alone."

"Don't go back there. It's in the past. Leave it there. Now tell me, why do you think Charisma is going to fall for you?"

He wasn't stupid. Dave knew his friend wanted him to forget about his past mistakes, and talking about Charisma was the only way he could do it. "I told you that she was halfway in love with me. I only need a little more time before she's completely mine."

"Maybe I need to warn this poor woman what she's getting into. I hate for someone as nice as Charisma to end up with you."

"Man…if I didn't know you were joking, I would be upset," Dave laughed, sending his previous problems to the back of his mind.

* * * *

"What crawled up your ass and died this afternoon? I got to take a longer lunch like you wanted," Charisma asked then took a sip of her iced tea.

"I'm sorry, but I'm worried about my father's business," Keira confessed, picking at the untouched food

146

on her plate. "He told me today that he's going to sell it to a complete stranger."

"Didn't you tell me that he's been really sick lately?" Charisma asked. "Maybe he's looking for a good person to take over the place since he knows that you aren't interested in the shop."

Keira rubbed the place between her eyebrows like she always did when she was upset about something. "How long have I known you?"

"Since Freshman year at college and we joined the sorority together. I thought you were crazy then, and I knew I had to become your friend."

"Hey… you were the one that ran past the library naked on a dare," Keira smirked. "Now who's the crazy one?"

"Shh….you weren't supposed to speak about that again," Charisma mumbled, looking around the small café. "I thought my mother would die when she had a meeting with the dean."

"I can still see that campus policeman giving you his jacket while trying not to look at your tattoo," Keira laughed, wiping tears away from her eyes with the back of her hands.

"Yeah…after he held it open for a good two minutes," Charisma snapped, remembering the bulky cop.

"Girl, if his eyes had popped out of his head anymore, he would have gone blind."

Charisma couldn't help but laugh harder at the memory. Keira was right. That that man had started at her so hard, she thought his eyes had crossed. "How did this conversation get turned back on me? I thought we are talking about you."

"Can we not discuss that?" Keira asked, sobering up. "I think my father's condition is worse than he's telling me."

Reaching across the table, Charisma covered her friend's coffee hand with her own. "Do you think he's dying?"

"Charisma, my dad smoked for ten years before he stopped, and he isn't the healthiest eater. That isn't going to take him away," Keira sighed rubbing that familiar spot on her face. "I can't lose him."

"Honey, you aren't going to lose your father. Mr. Winters is a tough man. He's going to be around for years."

"I hope so," Keira sighed. "Now tell me, how are things going with you and muscles? Has he gotten you to fall head over heels in love with him yet?"

Charisma felt a tingle in the direction of her heart as she thought about love and Dave in the same sentence. "He's growing on me."

"Don't you mean he grows longer and thicker when he sees you?"

"You're just plain nasty," Charisma giggled.

"Hey! I learned from the best."

"Can I ask you something?" Charisma questioned. "I know why I'm not married, but why are you still single?"

"It's the age old excuse. I'm waiting for the right man. I can't just settle down with anyone. It took True and Jenisha forever to fall in love and marry their husbands. Nevertheless, I'm not about to give up. I know he's out there for me. Look at how long it took you to find Dave?"

"Dave isn't mine," Charisma denied. "We're just friends and nothing else."

"Sure," Keira snickered, waving a waiter over to their table. "You keep telling yourself that."

"I'm done talking about Dave. I want to know more about this guy your father is selling his shop to. Have you met this guy?" Charisma was surprised that Keira was so upset about this. Her friend wasn't never interested in the motorcycle shop that her father owned, so why was it bothering her so much now?

"No, I'm supposed to meet him in a couple of weeks. Dad is drawing up some initial papers for him to look over."

"Don't judge this person before you see him. He might be the extra help your father needs right now." Charisma stopped talking when the waiter approached the table. She waited while Keira paid their bill." I don't like how down you are. Let's have dinner tonight. I talked to Jenisha before I got here and she told me that True is in town. We can make a night of it."

Keira rose from her seat and pushed the chair back under the table. "Are you sure that Dave wouldn't mind? Shouldn't you be spending time with him while he's here?"

"No, he's visiting an old friend," Charisma answered, standing up. "I'll just tell him I'm having a girl's night out and he'll understand."

"Sounds like Dave is your boyfriend," Keira teased, walking with her to the front doors and outside the restaurant.

Charisma shoved down the leap of emotions that settled in the middle of her chest at the thought of Dave being her boyfriend. They were only friends for the moment, and she couldn't let it go beyond that.

"Dave and I are only friends," she corrected. "We hang out and have a good time. I haven't thought about it growing into anything more serious than that." She wondered if Keira knew she was lying through her teeth. Dave was perfect for her, but she wasn't ready to take that big step yet.

"I hope Dave doesn't believe those lies. You may be able to fool him, but you aren't getting by that easy with me," Keira said, crossing her arms under her breasts. "You have more than 'friend feelings' for Dave. He's *the one*, and you know it."

Charisma opened and closed her mouth a several times trying to find a way to get Keira off her back, but she didn't know what to say. Dave was becoming an important part of her life. Somehow, he had charmed his sexy ass under her radar, and now she was clueless about what she was going to do about it.

"You're right on certain points, and wrong on others. I've feelings for Dave, but I doubt if we end up like our friends. I don't think marriage is in my future. Right now, I only want to enjoy the newness of everything with Dave. After it wears off, I'll have to see what happens."

"Have you talked to Dave about this?" Keira asked as she went towards her car parked at the end of the street with Charisma next to hers.

"Dave knows how I feel about him," she replied, avoiding the question. She wasn't ready to speak about her attachment to Dave yet. Everything was going great as it was. Why would she want to ruin it with sugar-coated words?

"I think you need to talk to him, because I hear he's falling for you," Keira informed her, unlocking her car door. She slid inside and closed it behind her.

Frowning, Charisma leaned inside the open window. "Who have you been talking to? Has Dave said something to you?"

"I can't tell my secrets. I'm just giving you the 411." Keira winked and started up her car as Charisma moved back.

"Keira Winters, you tell me who told you that," Charisma demanded stepping back. She had two guesses who her friend had been referring to and Mrs. Jenisha Campbell was going to get an ear full. Jenisha had to stop encouraging him all the time.

"I'm going to have a talk with Mrs. Campbell. She has to stop playing cupid and let me live my own life."

"I think it's sweet. She wants you to end up with your soul mate, and let me tell you, he's double damn fine," Keira grinned.

Charisma tried not to return the smile, but she couldn't. Keira had a way about her that she couldn't stay mad at her long. "Why don't you get out of here, and go check on your father. I've to get back to work before Lily moves into my office."

"Is that stripper wannabe still in your face?"

"Yes, she is," Charisma sighed. "She has to get me fired so she can start earning all that extra money for her hooker shoes."

"We are so bad."

Lifting her shoulder, she looked at her best friend inside the car looking too gorgeous in all white showing off the cocoa smoothness of her skin. "We're speaking the truth. You had the unfortunate opportunity to meet her, so you know it's the truth. I think you need a man."

"I can't get involved with anyone. Now isn't the time for a man in my life. Dad has to come first."

She heard the sorrow in Keira's voice and wished there was something that she could do. "Well…tonight we're going to throw all of problems behind us and enjoy a girl's night out."

"Where do you want to have this girl's night out?"

"It's going to be at my house. I thought about making it into a slumber party," Charisma replied. "I miss those days."

"I'll bring cookies and ice cream," Keira moaned, rolling her eyes. "I can already taste it."

"You and your sweet tooth," she laughed. Charisma remembered all those late night runs to the grocery store.

"Yeah, I better bring two boxes. I think it might not last long with True being pregnant and all."

Charisma loved how Keira, True, Jenisha and she had become such good friends over the past years. She didn't know what she would do without them. "Okay….I'll order pizza and some hot wings."

"Hot wings," Keira moaned, rubbing her stomach. "You're trying to make me fatter, aren't you?"

An innocent look suddenly plastered itself all over Charisma's face. "No, I want us to have fun. I'll fix the mixed drinks for us and Jenisha and True can enjoy Kool-aid."

"That's right. Little Mrs. True is pregnant again. How far along is she?"

"Six months, I believe, and Jenisha doesn't drink that often, so I doubt she'll want anything." Charisma glanced at down at her watch and groaned. She only had fifteen minutes to get back to work. "Keira, I've to go, but don't forget to be at my home by six o'clock."

"I'll be there with the ice cream, sprinkles, hot fudge, and anything else I can think of," Keira promised before she waved and pulled out into traffic.

Shaking her head, Charisma hurried across the street to her car and got inside. She went through several different radio stations until she found the one that she wanted. "How in the world did I end up with such a crazy friend?" she muttered to herself as she checked in the rearview mirror before driving off.

Chapter Nineteen

"Baby, I wanted to make dinner for you and introduce you to my sister today," Dave complained, wrapping his arms around her as he kicked the front door closed with the heel of his shoe. "I was going to make a special Filipino meal for you. I know you would have loved it."

Standing on tiptoes, Charisma kissed the hunk on the lips. It was so sad that this fake pouting act was getting to her, but she knew that Dave wouldn't mind if she spent the night with the girls. "Dave, I know you can find something to do for the rest of the day," she grinned, running her index finger down the bridge of his nose.

"How about you let me stay and show you what you're going to be missing tonight?" he suggested, moving her hand to cup his erection nestled between their bodies.

Slipping her hand into his gray gym shorts, Charisma trailed the length of Dave's cock with her fingers and brushed the tip with her thumb, producing a drop of moisture. "It hasn't been that long since we made love, has it? I'm sure you can make it another day," she teased, stroking him slowly.

"It has been days and you know it," Dave growled underneath his breath.

"Oh, has it?" Charisma replied sweetly as she continued to slide her hand up and down the thick length of Dave. She'll never forget how hard and thick he felt through her white slacks at Jenisha's house.

"Charisma," Dave moaned as his cock started to jerk in her hand.

"Yes, Dave?" she answered as she watched a fine coating of sweat build up on his muscular chest. "Are you having problems?"

"You aren't playing fair," he shivered as she made small circles over his large mushroom head with her thumb.

Charisma couldn't believe that Dave's cock was so large as muscular as his was. She had always thought that guys who worked out as much as him was lacking in the penis department, but Dave was proving her wrong.

"Why would you say that?" she asked, running her tongue over Dave's hard nipples and enjoying how his body jerked under her touch. She blew on it a couple of times and moved back. "I thought you enjoyed when I touched your body."

"I did... I do," he moaned, thrusting his erection against her damp palm.

"So, what's the problem?" she purred, running her free hand down the middle of his chest. "Do you want me to stop?" Charisma asked as she slowly started to release his erection finger by finger.

"No, don't," he panted placing her small hand back on him. "I can't go home like this. Baby, please. I'm hurting so bad." Chocolate eyes held hers as his hand showed the speed that would end the teasing game she started.

Charisma didn't want to be turned on, but she was. This would be the first time she would ever make a man orgasm just with her touch. "Is this how you like it?" she moaned as Dave dropped his hand and closed his sinful eyes.

Before Dave answered, his orgasm hit covering her fingers, and his cries shot through her empty house almost making her find her own release. She had never seen anything sexier in her entire life. She removed her wet hand from Dave's shorts and started to wipe it on the front of her shirt, but his hand shot out and stopped her.

"No, don't," he panted slowly, trying to regain his breath. "I want you to touch yourself."

"What?" she whispered, stunned. Charisma looked down at her dripping hand and back at Dave's face. The heat pouring from his eyes almost made her take a step back.

"I want to watch you touch yourself with the same hand that brought me pleasure," he whispered as his hand unbuttoned her slacks and pushed them down her legs. "Kick them away."

Totally lost in the moment that Dave was creating, Charisma used her bare feet to get her pants the rest of the way off and kicked them away from. Her pulse sped up as Dave wrapped his fingers around her wrist and brought her hand between her thighs. She was already dripping wet from watching him, and the thought of doing this would send her over the edge.

"Come on, baby, spread them wider for me," Dave coaxed, placing his free hand on her leg. "It's going to be so good."

Slowly, she opened her legs and gasped when Dave gently shoved two of her fingers inside of her wet core. "Oh, shit," she moaned as the touch of Dave's knuckles tickled her moist curls.

"Does it feel good?" he breathed by her ear, working her fingers in and out of her. "Wouldn't it feel better if it was me inside of you instead?"

Charisma was trying to bring herself out of the daze Dave was seducing her with. "You know we can't. I have the girls coming over." Shit, why did she even start this? His caress was making her crazy with need. She flinched as a thumb made circles around the part that wanted Dave the most. "Let me stay," a hot voice whispered. "I know the girls won't mind."

"I can't," she moaned as Dave continued to torment her with her own damn hand. *This wasn't fair!* He shouldn't be able to make her do this that she has never done with another man before.

"Are you sure?" he asked as the first signs of her orgasm started to hit her. It wouldn't be long until she exploded into a million pieces. "Do you really want me to leave?"

"Yes… I want you to leave."

"Don't say I never did as you asked," Dave said as he removed her hand and stepped back from her body. "Have fun with the girls tonight, and call me later."

Charisma stood shell shocked as Dave winked at her and strolled out the front door like he didn't have a care in the world. She wasn't able to get her words out of her mouth. Dave left her standing half-naked in her living room on the verge of an orgasm.

"I'm going to kill him the next time I see his sorry ass," she cursed, removing the rest her clothes as she headed to the bathroom. She needed a long shower to calm down, or she wouldn't be able to get through the party.

* * * *

Inside the shower, Charisma turned the water to a warmer temperature and let it work the tension from her neck and shoulders. She was still blown away by how she let Dave take control of her body. Just as she was reaching for the showerhead to wash the soap from her back, an arm wrapped around her and jerked her back against a hard chest.

A scream was working it was up her throat until she heard. "It's me, baby. Don't scream," Dave whispered by her ear. "Do you think I would really leave you like this?" Spinning her arm, he pressed her back against the wall and slipped a hard leg between her thighs.

"What are you doing here?" she finally questioned when she regained her breath.

"He missed you and wanted to come for a visit."

"He who?" she asked, staring into Dave's hypnotic eyes.

"Him," he growled, brushing his erection against her. "He wanted to know if he could come in and play for a little while."

The hot water from the shower pounded around them, making it into a private fantasy. Water dripped off Dave's wide shoulders and plastered his short black hair against his skull, making his handsome features stand out more. Charisma slowly realized that she was falling for the man positioned in front of her. He made things fun in and out of the bedroom, something that never has happened to her before. She wasn't ready to call it love, but it was.

"What if the playground is closed for the night?" she asked, enjoying the way Dave looked when he was hard and wet.

"I swear he'll make the after-hours play worth it," he countered, lifting her legs and wrapping them around his hips.

"I guess he can come in," she grinned, placing her arms around his neck. Charisma purred when Dave entered her with one sure stroke. "Damn, handsome, you were right. My playground was looking for a little after-hours visit from you."

"Good," Dave grinned as he braced one of his hands on the tile next to her head. "Now, let's make it worth it," he suggested, working his hips so his cock went as deep as possible.

Charisma lost her train of thought as Dave nibbled at her neck and the romance of the moment took her over. She wasn't going to be ready when Keira and the rest of the girls showed up. Right now, this was for her, and she was going to enjoy every *scrumptious* moment of it.

Chapter Twenty

Charisma snuggled closer to the warm body underneath her head and ignored the buzzing by her ear. Why would she want to answer that noise when her body was feeling so unbelievably good? Her mind couldn't think back to the last time she hadn't wanted to crawl out of bed.

"Babe, is that your alarm clock?" a warm deep voice asked by her head. "Aren't you supposed to be getting ready for your girl's night out?"

Opening her eyes, Charisma leaped up and her eyes swung down to Dave lying next to her in the rumbled bed. "Holy Shit, what am I doing still in bed with you?" she screamed, jumping up and grabbed her robe off the end of the bed. She shut off the alarm and groaned at the time. Keira and the rest of the women would be at her house in little over an hour and nothing was ready.

"You have to leave," Charisma exclaimed as she rushed over to her closet. "I need to take a shower and get dressed. I can't believe I let you do this to me."

"Now…I don't remember you telling me that when I brought our licking game into the bedroom," Dave countered, getting out of the bed. "However, I do recall you screaming my name out when I had my tongue inside your…" Dave stepped to the side when a pink slipper was flung at his head.

"I'm not playing with you," Charisma groaned, grabbing an outfit out of the closet, tossing it on the bed.

She glanced at Dave from the corner of her eye and noticed his ever-present erection.

"I know you don't think we're going to have sex again," she gawked waving her finger in his direction. "You better do something about that and quick. I'm already running late because of you."

One large shoulder shrugged as Dave reached out and grabbed her as she raced past him. "He likes you a lot. I never had this problem with other women, plus we don't have sex…we make love."

Charisma shook off the warm feeling Dave's words gave her. He was melting her heart more and more each day. "Handsome, I'm serious. You need to find your clothes and get them on. I still have to order the pizza and hot wings before they get here."

"How about I get dressed and order the food? I noticed some menus on your counter earlier and you can take your shower."

"Dave, you can't join me again, or I won't be ready in time."

"I kinda figure that out," he moaned, kissing her on the top of her head. "I better go and get dressed before I change my mind." Dave gave her another small kiss and headed out the door.

Against her will, Charisma twirled around and watched the most perfect ass she had ever seen on a man saunter from her bedroom. "It should be a crime for one man to look that good," she complained, leaving her bedroom and heading for the shower.

* * * *

Dave finished giving the young boy on the phone the order and tossed the cordless phone back down on the island. He couldn't stop the warm feeling that was sneaking its way into his body as he listened to Charisma sing off-key in the shower.

"I love her so much. I can't believe that I lasted this long without her in my life."

His personal life was going better than he ever thought possible. Charisma fit perfectly into everything that he wanted to do, and it was time to prove to her she wasn't wasting her time on him.

Resting his back against the counter, he thought about a way to approach Clinton about taking over the new CCD branch in Florida. He graduated at the top of his business and computer class. He could handle most of the office work, so the only thing he might need would be an assistant.

Charisma was so successful with everything that she did, and he didn't want to be what held her back. He wanted to carry his own weight when it came to their relationship. How could he even *think* about competing with most of the men she signed at the sports agency with his construction salary?

A woman like Charisma wanted to be shown the world. If he didn't hurry up and put his degree to use, it wasn't going to happen and another man could steal her away from him.

"I won't lose you to another man," Dave muttered, staring in the direction of Charisma's bedroom. "I've waited too long to find someone as extraordinary as you."

The sound of the doorbell dragged Dave away from his daydream and a grin spread across his face before he even went to answer the door. He already knew what trouble lay on the other side.

"Hello, Ladies," he grinned.

"Dave, what are you doing here?" Jenisha grinned back, switching the bag back and forth in her arms with True and Keira standing behind her.

Taking the bag from Jenisha, Dave stepped back and waved them in the house. "Come on in and have a seat. Charisma's back in the bedroom getting dressed."

"Is there a reason why she doesn't already have clothes on?" True asked, rubbing her stomach as she strolled in eyeing him.

"Now, I didn't think I would have to explain it to you since Hayward does the same thing to you," Jenisha laughed then winked at him.

"Ladies...stop teasing Charisma's man," Keira scolded as he took the bag of ice cream from her. "The two of you haven't forgotten those days since you've gotten married. True is proof that Hayward still likes to get freaky. Look. She's pregnant again with twins."

"Keira, I can't wait until you fall in love so we can tease you about it," Jenisha teased following True over to the couch.

"Ladies, I forgot how much fun it was being around all of you," Dave said as he placed the ice cream in the freezer and the bag on the table. "But I better go and find something to do with my night since I can't spend it with my Charisma."

"Your Charisma?" Keira asked, falling down into an oversized leopard chair.

Opening the front door, Dave looked back at the women that he loved like sisters and knew he couldn't wait until he officially became a part of the exclusive club. "Yeah...Charisma is mine, and I'm not going to ever give her up." He was on his way out the door when Jenisha's voice stopped him.

"Dave, Clinton went to Jim's house. I think they're going to play pool for a while and watch sports. Go on over there and keep them company."

"Thanks. I'll check in with those knuckleheads, and I'll be sure to let Clinton know that I left you here with your crazy friends." Dave quickly closed the door before he heard any comments.

Dave was halfway to his black truck when he heard his name being yelled behind him. Pivoting, he smiled when his eyes landed on Charisma closing her front door before she ran up to him.

"Where you really going to leave without telling me goodbye?" she pouted, looking too cute in her pink shorts and matching T-shirt.

He was very glad no men were going to be at this slumber party, because he couldn't take his eyes off the way shirt cupped Charisma's full breasts. She looked amazing with her short hair spiked up a little. The newer looked added a glow to her topaz eyes. Hell, he was so in love with this woman, and they only had been one official date.

"Babe, I didn't think I'd be able to keep my hands off of you inside the house, so I decided to leave instead," he confessed, brushing his knuckles down the side of her face.

Tilting her head, Charisma let her eyes travel the length of his body before speaking. "I see you have your shirt out. Did you not get rid of that problem you had in the bedroom earlier?"

"Charisma...don't you start with me," Dave growled, yanking the cute minx to his chest. "I need to leave before I do something neither one of us has time for."

"Like what?" she purred, licking her lips, running her hands down his chest until she cupped his cock in the palm of her hand. "The girls are looking at my DVDs deciding on which one to watch."

Dave didn't need a second invitation. He quickly unlocked his truck door and ushered Charisma inside, slamming it shut behind them. Without giving her a second to catch her breath, he lifted up Charisma so she straddled his thighs and yanked the T-shirt over her head.

His lips latched on her full right breast while he used his right hand to play with the other one. Moaning deep in her throat, Charisma wrapped her hands around his head and pressed his face even closer.

"Hmmmm…" she panted, rocking her hips over his hard as granite cock. "We shouldn't be doing this. I need to go."

Moving his head, Dave licked his tongue across the perfect nipples staring at him in the face. "In a minute….I want a small taste." Before Charisma could move, he eased his hand inside of her shorts and inserted two fingers inside of her dripping core. Removing them, he placed them in his mouth and sucked them clean. "Sweeter than any honey I've ever tasted."

Blinking a couple of times, Charisma stared at him until a huge grin passed across her face. "You're so bad, and I need to stop hanging around you," she teased as she grabbed her shirt off the passenger seat. She pulled it over her head and straightened it back up. "Stay out of trouble, and I'll talk to you later." She climbed across his lap and reached for the passenger's side door.

"Why later?" Dave asked, grabbing Charisma by the arm. "I want to see you tomorrow. It's my last day in California, and I want to spend it with you."

"Handsome, I can't. I've a new client coming to the office, and I'll be there most of the day. I won't have a moment to spare for anyone," she complained, glancing over her shoulder. "I need to get him to sign on the dotted line, or Lily will take my job."

He let go of Charisma's arm like he had been burnt. Dark brown eyes turned hard as he looked at her. "Are you telling me that you rather spend time with another man instead of me?"

"Dave, it's my job. I don't have a say in it. Mr. Thurman is making everyone come in to work on their client roster. Please understand. If I could get away, I would."

"Who is this person you're going to be working so closely with? Do I know him?"

"Ross Ferguson."

"Ross Ferguson? The star quarterback of the Providers?" Dave snapped, barely able to control his growing temper. "Isn't he the same guy you blew me off for in Jamaica?"

"Yes, but it was business then, too," Charisma replied. Reaching to touch his arm, he jerked it away.

"Are you fucking him?"

Charisma sprung back from him like he had shoved her. "What did you just say?" she hissed. "I know I heard you wrong."

He didn't move his eyes from her face. Dave knew it wasn't a possibility that Charisma was sleeping with another man, but he couldn't stop the words from pouring from his mouth. "I asked were you sleeping with him. I've heard how easy it is for football players to get women to drop their panties for them."

Dave congratulated himself from not flinching when Charisma slapped him. "You son of a bitch," she screamed. "How dare you ask me something like that after what we just shared inside and outside! I don't know what kind of women you've dated in the past, but I only sleep with one man at a time."

Opening the door, she climbed out and stared back in at him, "I think it would be best if you lost my number and forgot my name, Dave Turner. I've enough going on without adding a two hundred and ninety-eight pound weight to my back," Charisma yelled, slamming the truck's door.

"Fuck!" Dave cursed as he got out of the driver's side and tried to stop Charisma before she got back into the house. He caught by her arm in the middle of the pathway.

"Sweetheart, I'm sorry. I don't know made me say that. Chalk it up to me being a jealous boyfriend."

"Let go of me," she retorted, pulling at his light grip. "I'm done talking to you. You aren't going to ruin tonight for me. I haven't had time with my girlfriends in a while."

He slowly released her and took a step back. "Okay, how about I catch a later flight back tomorrow, and we can have a late dinner?"

"I'm not going to have dinner with you tomorrow or any other time. Furthermore, you aren't my boyfriend. You're just a mistake that I want to try my best to forget. Go home, Dave." Charisma hurried in the house and closed the door softly behind her.

Crap! Dave took a step towards Charisma's front door and changed his mind. He wouldn't be able to talk to her with all of her girlfriends in there. They would be on her side and not give him a chance to explain himself. Maybe it would be for the best if he went back home and gave Charisma a few days to cool off. Dave made his way back to his truck and thought about going back to the hotel, but changed his mind at the last minute. He might know someone who could help him out.

* * * *

"Whoa…I can't believe you asked Charisma if she's sleeping with that football player," Clinton laughed then shoved another chip into his mouth.

"It not funny," Dave growled, taking another swallow of his beer. "Do you know that she told me not to come back?"

"Good riddance is all I can say," Jim chimed in then took his shot.

"Just because you having problems with your ex-wife doesn't mean I'm going to give up on women," he replied, sitting his beer down on the counter. "I've wanted to be with Charisma since the first time I laid eyes on her."

"I know how that feels," Clinton agreed. "Jenisha was everything I wanted and still is."

"The two of you make me so sick. How can you let these women rule you like this? I'm not wasting my time on them again. I'm going to focus my time on my work and my son."

"Jim, stop complaining and think of a way to help me out. I want Charisma, and my big mouth may have cost me the woman I'm falling in love with," he groaned. Dave finished off one beer and reached for another one.

"Big guy, you need to slow down on those," Clinton said, nodding to the beer in his hand. "Or you won't be able to drive back to the hotel tonight."

"He's not driving. I'm going to let him crash in the spare bedroom," Jim stated, laying down his pool stick. "Hand me your hotel key, and I'll go and pick up your stuff."

"No, I'll be fine," Dave said with a shake of his head. "I can make it back there just fine."

"I'm not asking twice. I know you've at least had four of those since you stomped through my front door. Hand me the key and let me go so I can get back. Keep Clinton company while I'm gone. Ask him about those kids of his."

Dave reached in his pocket and tossed Jim the key to his room. "Thanks man. I'll leave early tomorrow and turn the room key back in before my flight."

"Not a problem," Jim said as he went out the door, closing it behind him.

"I can't wait until he falls in love. I'm going to tease the hell out of him," Clinton laughed, then sobered up at the distraught look on Dave's face.

"Dave, Charisma is going to forgive you. Do you want me to call Jenisha and have her talk to her for you?"

"No, I'm going to give her some space like she asked. But I do have something that I want to discuss with you," he answered, sliding his beer away from him.

"What's up?" Clinton asked.

"I know that CCD is opening up a firm in Florida, and I was wondering could I get a job there. I've taken all the necessary classes to get interviewed for one of the office positions."

"Hayward was talking about you the other day and a position that he thought would be a perfect match for you. Let me see what he was thinking about, and I'll call you when you get back home."

"Thanks. I'd like that. I want to prove that I can do more than be the muscles on a construction site."

"Are you doing this for someone special?"

"In one word, Charisma," Dave replied, thinking about how she looked at him before she raced back in the house. He never wanted to see that look on her face again. "I've to prove to her that I'm worth her time and energy."

"Has she said something to you about your job?" Clinton frowned. "I didn't think she would do something like that."

"Charisma hadn't said a word to me, but I want to be able to take her to an expensive restaurant or buy her a present without wondering if it's good enough."

Chuckling, Clinton reclined back in his seat and shook his head. "You'll learn soon enough if she truly loves you. None of that will matter. But I think you might have a bigger problem looming in your future."

"What problem?"

"Trish. She called my office looking for you yesterday."

"SHIT!" Dave groaned. "I thought she understood it was over between us."

"I guess not. I never got the relationship that you had with her, but you need to tell Charisma, or it will blow up in your face. I'm speaking from experience."

"I know," he sighed, running his hand over his hair. "But I don't know how to approach it. I'm trying my best to keep that part of my life in the past."

"When you try to hide things from the people you love, it always has a way coming out in the open. My mother told us that what you do in the dark will eventually come out in the light," Clinton preached at him. "You need to tell Charisma about Jackson and Trish now and not later."

Dave hated when Clinton acted more like his father than his friend. He didn't want to listen to this tonight. All he wanted to do was drown his sorrows. "I hear you, but I just can't tell her yet. I'll confess when the time is right."

"Don't wait too long, or you'll regret it more than you'll ever know."

"Pray that I don't," Dave flung back and then finished his lukewarm beer in hopes of forgetting his horrible comments to Charisma.

Chapter Twenty-One

"I never knew airports could be so damn loud," he moaned, holding his head begging for the noise to stop. "I can't take this. How am I going to be able to deal with a flight?"

"I told you last night to stop drinking, but you didn't listen to me. If Clinton hadn't stayed longer, I wouldn't have been able to move your big ass off my couch," Jim complained, flicking the side of Dave's head with his finger. "You deserve the pain you're in getting upset over a woman. I'll admit Charisma is cute, but she isn't worth all of this."

Dave slowly opened his eyes then cursed as the light made another pain shoot through his head. "Charisma is breathtaking, and I want to marry her, but I might have ruined my chances."

"Marry her?" Jim sputtered. "Have you lost your mind? What has gotten into you? Next thing I know, you'll be having a house full of kids like Hayward and Clinton."

"I want kids, so shut up. Don't you love the hell out of Trevor?"

"Trevor is my world, and I would do anything for my son," Jim answered.

"Good…then you know how…" Dave wasn't able to finish because of the slap across the back of his head. He flinched and spun around ready to fight until he looked up. Shit, he didn't need this early as it was.

"Dave…I can't believe you. How could you do that to Charisma?" Keira yelled at him and stomped around his chair.

"Keira, my head is killing me. Could you please not yell at me?" he groaned, staring up at her. "I told her I was sorry, but she didn't want to hear me."

"You accused her of sleeping with another man, and you think saying a tired old 'I'm sorry' will fix your idiot mistake?" Keira snapped underneath her breath. "I've never seen my best friend that upset before."

Dave eyed Keira's flight attendant's uniform and sighed. This was going to be the longest flight back home of his life. "You're on this flight, aren't you?"

"Yes, and you better not look at me the wrong way, or I'll make you wish you took another flight."

He wasn't surprised that Keira was disappointed by the way he treated Charisma last night, but what stunned him was how passionate she was about it. "Keira, I would never do anything to hurt my Charisma. It just got out of hand, and things were said that shouldn't have been."

"Things were said... is that your dumb ass excuse? Has Charisma ever insulted you like that?" Keira questioned, folding her arms under her breasts looking very protective of her friend. Despite his killer headache, Dave had to smile at the how she cute looked. He could take her without even trying. She was so small compared to him. Charisma really had a wonderful friend in Keira.

"No. Charisma hasn't been anything but a sweetheart to me," he confessed, rubbing his throbbing temple.

"Why don't you stop with all the questions? Don't you see that he doesn't feel good?" Jim's rough voice demanded next to him.

* * * *

Swinging her head to the left, Keira stared at the man sitting next to Dave and tried not to let her mouth hang open in shock. He was almost the same build as Dave, but without the same bulk. Dark brown hair that looked almost black until the lights hit in certain areas was pulled back into a long ponytail that went below his shoulders.

Eyes that looked bluer than green glared up at her with an expression that made her narrow her own. A goatee was neatly trimmed around firm looking lips. Usually she hated facial hair on men, but it only added to this guy's sex appeal. There was no doubt that this guy was gorgeous, but the bad side of it was that he knew it, too.

"Who are you, Dave's bodyguard?" she questioned. "I think he's big enough and old enough to take care of himself."

"Listen, chick. I don't think Dave needs to hear you criticize him about Charisma. The two of them are having a little fight, but they'll work it out. So why don't you stay out of it?"

Keira never in her life felt so insulted. She almost lost her ability to speak for a few seconds. "Chick," she sputtered. "I have a name and chick isn't it. Besides, I wasn't talking to you."

"I know you weren't, but Dave is too nice to tell you to shut up and mind your own damn business," the man flung back at her.

"Who in the hell is this man?" she questioned, looking back at Dave who was looking at her and the man with an amused expression on his face.

"Jim Russell, meet Keira Winters," Dave said, pointing a thumb in the guy's direction sitting next to him. "Keira Winters, meet my best friend Jim Russell. I apologize. He isn't usually that rude."

"I'm not worried about him. What I am concerned about is you and Charisma. I think you're perfect for her, but this jealousy is totally uncalled for. I've know Charisma since our freshman year of college, and she would never cheat on a guy."

The sound of their plane been announced to board finally got Keira to stop giving him the third degree. She gave him another look of disbelief then spun on her heel and headed for the plane.

* * * *

"Hell... I'm glad that I don't have to be around her all of the time. Is she always so damn opinionated?" Jim complained, staring at the back of Keira.

"No, Keira is usually pretty laid back, so I must have really hurt Charisma for her to confront me like that. Maybe I should stay and talk to her," Dave replied, staring at Keira in the distance as she spoke with other flight attendants.

"I wouldn't do it. I can only imagine how pissed your woman is if Keira was acting like that," Jim grumbled, standing up. "We better go. It looks like that line is getting longer and longer."

"Alright, but I'm going to call Charisma as soon as I get back home. I can't let her think that I don't regret what I said to her. She's *the one*, and I'm not about to lose her over something stupid."

Dave got up and walked beside Jim until Jim couldn't go any further with him. He gave his friend a quick hug then stepped back. "Jim, I know you mean well, but Charisma means the world to me. I'm not going to let her go without a fight. Keira had all the right to jump in my face. Charisma is special, and I should treat her like that."

Jim gave him a 'don't bother with her' look, but he blew it off. His friend wasn't in love, and when he was, he would understand everything he was going through. "Stop giving me that look. You're having a bad spell at the moment. But when it's over, you'll be coming back to me for advice."

"I never came to you for advice about women. God, in the past, the girls you dated couldn't spell the word advice. I'll never understand what Charisma sees in you, or should I say saw in you?"

Dave gave his friend a playful shove and hurried away from him. "I can't stand here and deal with you. I have to go, or I'm not going to make it back home on this flight."

He didn't miss the look that passed across Jim's face. "Have fun with Keira. I'm lucky it isn't me that has to deal with her."

* * * *

Pressing the button for a third time, Dave watched as Keira waltzed past him like he hadn't even asked for her assistance. He had to find out what was going on with Charisma before he called her. She probably wasn't going to answer the phone, but he had to give it a try. Charisma was just so damn flawless in every sense of the word, and sometimes he forgot that he couldn't keep a tight leash on her. Her job involved her being around talented men that most women would find attractive, and that was something he had to deal with.

"Keira, can you please stop and speak with me?" he asked as she stormed past him again.

Spinning around, Keira came back and glared at him. "What is it, Dave?"

"How's Charisma doing? I tried calling her before I left, but she wouldn't answer. I left messages and she hasn't returned any of them. I'm truly sorry for what I said. I should get a degree for sticking my foot in my mouth."

Keira's face softened a little at his words. "Dave, I'm going to tell you something, and if you breathe a word of it to Charisma, I'll kill you."

Dave chuckled at the thought of Keira trying to hurt him. She might be taller than his Charisma, but she didn't look any stronger, in his opinion. "I swear I won't say a word," he promised.

"Charisma is falling in love with you. You're all she talks about. This look comes across her face when your name is mentioned."

"Has she told you that?"

"No, but it's only a matter of time. She tells me everything." Keira glanced over his head and nodded. "I've to go, but remember what I told you," she said and started to move away from him.

"Keira, wait."

"Yes?" she answered, looking about over her shoulder.

"Thank you."

"You're welcome. I like you, and I think you're just the man Charisma needs in her life." Keira gave him a small smile and headed over to another passenger.

"I'm the one and only man for Charisma Miles, and I'm going to prove it to her," Dave swore as he reached for the magazine in front of him.

Chapter Twenty-Two

"You don't look good. Did your trip go badly? I thought you would come back with a smile a mile long since you were going to see your woman," Brittney commented and popped her grape gum before falling down into a chair by his bed.

"What makes you think I was going to see a woman?" Dave questioned as he dumped his dirty clothes into a pile so he could put them in the washing machine later. "I went to visit Clinton about a business matter."

"Sure you did. I heard you on the phone asking about Charisma. I know that you're dating her, so when I do I get to meet her and what is Trish going to say about this? You know how attached she is to you."

Dave flung his baby sister a hard look before he grabbed his empty suitcase off the bed and placed it back inside his walk-in closet. How in the world did Brittney know so much about his life when she was seldom around him? Did she have ESP or something?

"Trish has nothing to do with my relationship with Charisma. She's just a good friend and nothing else. She understands that, and I won't let you meet Charisma until you learn some respect."

"Hey, I'm respectful to older people," his sister complained, plunking her gum into the trashcan by the chair. "I promise that I won't do anything to embarrass you. Do you think I'm going to tell her about your past?"

"I told you not to bring that up again. Shit, that was years ago. How do you know so much about what I did when I was younger?"

"Mom and Dad really shouldn't think I am asleep when they were arguing about sending me to spend time with you. I heard about all the crazy things that you did before I was born. I still can't believe you were in the military and left after your time was up. Why didn't you reenlist?"

Dave didn't want to discuss the time he served in the Army with his baby sister. It was a part of his life that he wanted to leave in the past. He made a lot of good friends there and lost contact with them over the years. He was glad he learned sooner than later a military life wasn't the career he wanted.

"Stop with all the questions, or I'm going to start asking some of my own," he threatened.

"Like what?" Brittney retorted, brushing her long blonde hair over her shoulder. He still hated that she dyed her naturally black hair blonde. She was so much like their mother in so many ways, and he prayed that she outgrew it. She was in her last year of high school and instead of looking eighteen, Brittney looked twenty-five. Men were taking notice of her too.

"Why aren't you out with Lindsey tonight? I thought the two of you were best friends. You stayed at her house while I was out of town. The two of you aren't ever apart."

"I can't stand that bitch anymore," Brittney snapped.

"Watch your language!" He wasn't fond of how his sister talked sometimes. She could be really agreeable one minute and in the next, she was a totally different girl.

"Sorry," she mumbled. "But Lindsey knew I wanted Carlson to ask me to the beach party tonight, and that slut got him to take her instead. I don't want to ever speak to her again."

Laughing, Dave had forgotten what it was like to be his sister's age and anytime something happened to you, it was the end of the world. Brittney had a lot of growing up to do and so many more things to experience out of life.

"How about I take you to the movies and out for something to eat afterwards?"

Brittney's face lit up like a two-year-old's on Christmas day. "Can we go see the new Transformers movie? Josh Duhamel is so hot."

"I guess so," he sighed.

"Plus, I want to go to *Riley's Pizza and More* that's right next door and none of those veggie pizzas that you're always ordering. I want sausage and pepperoni with double cheese and a pitcher of cola."

Was Brittney trying to ruin his workout routine? He hadn't eaten stuff like that in such a long time. "Can't I order you that and get my regular veggie pizza?"

"Nope," she ginned. "Big brother, you're built like a house. I know cheating tonight isn't going to add an ounce of fat to your sculptured body. Live a little."

"I'll do this if you clean up your room first thing tomorrow morning. I can't believe you sleep in there," Dave complained. "It's worse than mine was at your age."

"Fine," Brittney groaned under her breath.

"No, not fine. Either you say 'Yes, Dave,' or we aren't going anywhere."

"Yes, Dave. I promise to clean up my room first thing in the morning. Now, can we go?"

"Yeah," he smiled at the sour look on his sister face and wondered if he really drove his parents this crazy when he was eighteen. "Let's get going, because I've no clue when this movie starts."

Brittney jumped out of the chair and raced out of the room and down the stairs. Dave snatched his car keys off the stand by his bedroom door and followed his sister. He couldn't wait until Brittney met Charisma. Between the two of them, they had enough energy to keep him on his toes forever.

* * * *

"Do you want to do this another time? I don't mind coming back, because your mind seems a million miles away."

Charisma looked up from the contract in front of her and stared at Ross Ferguson sitting across from her. The side of his mouth was pulled into a gentle smile as he gazed back at her. He was a very handsome guy, but she wished Dave was there in front of her instead. She still was trying to recover from Keira's report of seeing him at the airport.

A small part of her was hurt that he didn't find a way to see her before he hopped on a plane and went back home. However, she wasn't going to lose Ross as a client because of it. She had to get her mind back on the task at hand.

"Please accept my apology, Mr. Ferguson. I didn't mean to space out on you like that. Have you had a chance to read over the contract? Does everything look in order to you?"

"I looked over it with my lawyer, and everything was in perfect order. I signed it last night. So, as of this moment, you're my sports agent. How about we go out and celebrate?" Ross suggested, giving her his million-dollar winning camera smile.

"Don't you remember that I told you I don't date my clients?" she answered, placing the contract into a folder by her elbow.

"I'm not considering this a date. I only wanted to go over a few things with you while we had a nice dinner. I know you're in love with that guy from Jamaica. "

"I'm not in love with Dave," she sputtered, thrown by Ross' comment. What made him think she was in love with Dave Turner? They were only friends, and nothing more.

"You're more than friends. I saw the way you couldn't stop looking at him. Besides, you aren't flirting with me, which means you have feelings for that guy. Does he know how lucky he is? If you were single, I wouldn't stop until you were my girlfriend."

"Maybe I'm just not interested in dating you, and that's why I'm not flirting with you," Charisma laughed at Ross' boyish charm. She now saw why he had so many adoring female fans. He knew how to spread it on thick.

"Nope. I'm not going to believe a word coming out of those gorgeous lips. You're in love with Dave. Hey, I'm a good guy, and I won't try to steal you from him. But if he ever loses his mind and lets you go, you have my number," Ross flirted, standing up and extended his hand

Grinning, Charisma stood up and shook Ross's hand. "I'll keep that in mind, Mr. Ferguson. However, if you have any other questions that deal with the contract, please contact me."

"Can't I get you to call me Ross?"

"I don't think that would be a good idea since you're signed with me now. I want to keep everything as professional as possible," Charisma stated, removing her hand. Ross was very attractive, and she might have gone out on a date or two with him if it was another time or place.

"Fine. I'll respect your wishes. But don't think I'm not a little envious you're taken." Ross grinned at her one last time before he strolled out the door.

Collapsing back into her seat, Charisma kicked off her shoes and rested her feet on top of her desk. Most of the staff was out to lunch, so she was going to take this free time and enjoy the peace and quiet. She couldn't keep down her bubble of happiness at signing Ross.

He was definitely going to help her chances at saving her job. Mr. Thurman had to see she was an important part of this firm now. Lily might be sleeping with him, but when it came down to this, Easton Thurman wanted money rolling into the corporation.

"I wouldn't get too happy at my desk. It doesn't matter you just signed Ross Ferguson on your roster. I'm still going to take your job and this office. You better enjoy it while you have it," the snippy tone hissed from her opened doorway. Charisma didn't have to move her head to know who said those words.

"Lily, shouldn't you be out sucking someone?" Charisma retorted. "Oh, sorry. I meant sucking up to someone? Slip of tongue."

"You bitch," Lily snapped. "Don't get all high and mighty on me. You aren't worth my time or breath, but I have to deal with you until I find a way to get you out of here. I still can't believe Easton hired you. Shouldn't you be out frying chicken at a restaurant or dating a basketball player?"

Charisma slowly dropped her legs and slipped her feet into her shoes. Getting up, she walked over to Lily until not one inch separated them. She had to give the younger woman credit. She wanted to run, but she didn't.

"First, I graduated at the top of my class, and I don't date basketball players just to get myself on television. Lily, you would do that, not me, because you're desperate and needy for attention. Lastly, I'm not going to ever address the chicken comment because it's old and played out. However, you have exactly two seconds to get out of my office, or I'll toss you and your Jimmy Choo knockoffs out."

"I'm going to tell Easton you threatened me," Lily warned. "He'll fire you."

"I'll report him for sleeping with one of his employee and firing me to give you the job, because you're good at using your mouth, and I don't mean for talking," Charisma threatened back. "Who do you think would be right out the door behind me, Miss Lily Kane?"

"You're going to get yours," Lily shouted. She spun on her five inch heels and stormed out the door.

"Not before you get yours for being the horrible person that you are!" Charisma yelled at her nemesis and slammed the door shut. "Please, Lord, give me strength not to kill that dim-wit."

Hearing her cell phone ring, Charisma raced back over to her purse and pulled it out. "Charisma Miles speaking." She could barely keep the anger out of her voice. Lily was driving her up the damn wall.

"Charisma, are you okay?" Keira questioned, worried. "I never heard you answer your phone like that before. Is it Dave?"

"I wish it was him instead of that evilness I work with," Charisma replied.

"Lily? What has she done now?"

"I can't get into it over the phone. How about I fix dinner at my house tonight and tell you and Jenisha all about it?"

"Sounds good to me," Keira agreed. "Are you sure Jenisha will be able to come? What about True? Is she still in town?"

"Anytime she can leave Clinton with the kids, she does. Besides, he loves it," she laughed. "He's such a Mr. Mom. Unfortunately, True can't. She caught a flight back to Montana this morning."

"He would die if he heard you call him that."

"I got it from Jenisha. She calls him that all the time, so can you call her with the details, and she can bring her delicious chocolate chip cookies. I need to eat something fattening tonight."

"Will do, and I'll see you around six o'clock?" Keira asked.

"Six is fine with me, because I'm leaving work around four o'clock."

"Bye, Charisma."

"Later, Keira," Charisma replied and disconnected the call, and put her phone back into her purse. She couldn't wait until tonight, being around her girlfriends always made her feel better.

Chapter Twenty-Three

"Dave, what are you doing here?" Trish asked, stepping back from the door. She held it open wider so he could come in. "I wasn't expecting to see you until next week." She kissed him on the cheek and closed the door behind him. "Have a seat. Do you want to stay for dinner?"

"I'd rather stand. What I have to say won't take that long," Dave exclaimed. "I've found someone, and I'm in love with her. I'm going to ask her to marry me as soon as I get the chance."

"No, you can't do this to me….to us. You promised that you would always be here for me. I won't let you do this," Trish cried, hitting him in the middle of his chest with the palms of her hands.

"I know what I promised, but this has to end. You've to move on with your life. Trish, you're a gorgeous woman, and if you get out there, any man would be crazy not to want you." He grabbed Trish's hands and held them away from his body. "You knew that we wouldn't be together forever."

"Yes, we are. I'm not going to let you brush me under the rug. You're mine, and you're going to stay with me."

"Trish, be reasonable. You had to know I was bound to fall in love one day and leave you. I never made any promises that we would end up as a couple," Dave spoke gently as if he was talking to a small child. "It's time to let the past go."

"You bastard," Trish shrieked, snatching her arms away from him. "Does this new love of your life know all about the skeletons in your closet?"

"I've not told her yet."

Laughing, Trish rubbed her wrists as she circled his body. "Do you really think she'll want you after she finds out what you did? I doubt it."

"Charisma is an understanding woman, and she'll forgive me for the wrong I've done in the past. I know she will." Dave silently prayed that Charisma would understand and not leave him.

"I'll save a place for you at the table, because you'll be back." Trish opened the front door for him and waved him out.

"I'm sorry, Trish. I hoped things could have turned out differently, but they can't." He paused by Trish and ran the back of his hand down the side of her face. "Goodbye," Dave murmured and dropped his hand. He spun on his heel and headed for his truck parked by the curb.

* * * *

"Are you hiding from me? Why haven't you answered any of my phone calls?" a voice challenged from her opened doorway early the next morning. "I had to come all the way back here just to make you talk to me. I'm really adding up the frequent flyer miles."

Laying her pen down, Charisma looked up and found Dave standing there looking better than the dream she had about him last night. He was wearing worn jeans with a dark green T-shirt molding the parts of his body she loved the best. "I have been too engaged to return any phone calls. I was going to call you later this afternoon," she said, avoiding maintaining eye contact with him.

"Liar," Dave taunted, advancing on her behind the desk. "You didn't have any plans to call me today or anytime in the near future. Did you think by not calling I wouldn't want to see your beautiful face, or I'll give up on what we have?"

Laying a palm on the flat surface, Dave leaned in closer to her personal space, filling her nose with his sexy cologne mingled with masculinity. "You are playing hard to get, and I find that so hot."

"I'm not playing hard to get. I'm just busy trying to save my job. Anyways, after the way we left things, I wasn't dying to return your calls. Your accusations were unwanted and uncalled for," she retorted, moving her head away. "I might not want you in my life anymore."

"Charisma, you are a like a puzzle missing the last piece to make it complete, and you will learn soon enough I'm the lost piece you have been searching for," he confessed, capturing her lips in a gentle kiss.

Moaning lightly, Charisma tried ignoring Dave, but instead she loved the tenderness of the kiss. She was supposed to be mad at him, but all she could think about was how she wished they could go back to her house.

Separating their lips, Dave said, "Say yes."

Still trapped in the sensual kiss Charisma whispered, "Yes."

"Wonderful. I'll pick up at seven thirty," he told her, easing away from her chair.

He was almost out the door before his words registered in her dazed mind. "Hey, what did I just commit myself to?"

"Our make-up date," Dave yelled back in the room.

Charisma fell back into the chair touching her still-swollen lips. "I won't let you be that missing piece."

Five minutes later, her phone rung and she picked it up. "Charisma Miles speaking. How may I help you?"

"Wear something fun and sexy," Dave said before he quickly disconnected the call.

Grinning, Charisma placed the phone back into its cradle. She hated to admit it, but Dave did make her smile and laugh more than any other man she had known. He was like the breath of fresh air she had been waiting for.

"I'm not going to let this get out of hand. We're only friends who enjoy each other's company. Nothing more will come from this," she promised herself. Now if she only believed it.

* * * *

"Have I told you how breathtaking you look tonight in that little black dress? Are you trying to make me jealous?" Dave inquired, gazing at her in the semi-dark bar. "I've noticed how the men in here can't take their eyes off of you."

"I'm here with you and not them. So I don't care what they're doing," Charisma replied, not knowing how her words stroked Dave's ego. "I want us to work through things, because I love being in your company. However, we have to set a few ground rules."

"Ground rules?" Dave groaned, not caring for the turn this conversation was taking.

Charisma continued liked she never heard a word he said. "First rule, you need to stop with the caveman jealousy. I'm not a piece of property to be fought over. Got it?"

Seconds clicked away while Dave contemplated the first rule. "Fine, I understand. I'll try to watch my jealousy. But if you weren't so hot, I wouldn't get jealous of other men when they looked at you."

"Men are going to look, but you should know me well enough by now to understand I don't cheat. Now, let's move on to the second rule."

"There's another rule?" Dave complained a moment before he took a sip of his drink. Sitting the glass back down, he ran his hand down his face. "Did your old relationships have to deal with all of these rules?"

"No," she chuckled.

"Then why do I have to follow so many?"

"Because I didn't care about them the way I do you," Charisma confessed. She knew Dave wouldn't give her any problems now, especially after her confession.

"I care about you, too, baby, and I'll be more than happy to follow your rules. When two people are in love, they do things for each other. Fire away the next rule and I promise that I'll handle it without flinching."

"You're in love with me?" Charisma sputtered. "That isn't possible. Maybe you need to stop talking nonsense."

The loud chatter in the room blocked out the sound of her heart pounding in her ears. She couldn't let Dave know she was falling in love with him, too. She had to stay focused on signing a couple of more people to her roster. Lily needed to be taught a lesson and she was the person that could do it.

"Don't be scared. I'm not trying to force you into saying the words back to me. Just know when you're ready, I'm here."

Charisma glanced at down as Dave's large hand engulfed hers on the table. *She was in love with this guy. Shit, what was she going to do now?* She needed to talk to Jenisha and fast. "I'm not scared. I'm just saying I like you the best out of all of the men I've been with. You're the most …" she stopped talking when Dave squeezed her hand lightly.

Shaking his head lightly, he said. "Don't compare me to the men from your past. They're in your past for a reason, and I want them to stay there. They have nothing to do with us."

Charisma didn't know what to say. Dave was so open and honest with his feelings about her. She wasn't used to this, and honestly, it was freaking her out a little. "I'll try not to bring up my past anymore and just focus on us."

"Good…how about we finish up this meal and hit the road? I've to help my sister with a school project. She's very good a blowing things off to the very last minute. I think she gets it from our mother."

"I'm always hearing about this sister of yours. When am I going to get to meet her?"

"Let me check and make sure she isn't doing anything this weekend, and I'll invite you over for dinner. Hell….if she is doing something, how about you come anyway?"

"You want me to come all the way to Florida for dinner?" Charisma gasped. "Isn't that a bit much?"

"I'm in love with you, and I'm going to do everything in my power to make this long distance thing work. But you've got to do your part, too," Dave stated. "I'll set everything up with the tickets and you can stay at my house."

"I'm not sure about that."

"Don't worry. As much as I love having your sexy body next to mine in the morning, I'll make up the guest room for you. Brittney is mature, but I don't want her knowing about my sex life."

"Are you saying you can stay out of my room?"

"Leave the door unlocked, and I'll be sure to give you a good night kiss," he whispered and winked.

"You're going to get me into a world of trouble, but I guess I can come see you. Are you sure that Brittney won't mind me just showing up?"

"Brittney is dying to meet you. She wants to know who has me traveling back and forth to California all the time. Anyway, it's past time she gets to know the woman I'm in love with."

"Dave, you know you make it really hard for me not to tell you how much I love you, too," Charisma whispered, finally ready to admit her feelings. She was in love and was no longer afraid to shout it out loud.

Standing up, Dave tossed a handful of bills on the table. "Come on, let's go," he said as he came around the table. He tugged her up from her seat and pulled her out of the restaurant behind him.

"What are you doing? Are we going to stay for dinner?" she exclaimed, almost running to keep up with his long strides. Had she made a mistake finally telling Dave how she felt about him?

"No, we aren't staying for dinner," he answered, as they got closer to his truck. "How do you expect me to stay in there after what you told me?" Placing her body against the driver's side of his truck, he boxed her body in with his. "Tell me again. I want to hear the words."

"I don't know what you mean," Charisma whispered as it finally dawned on her how her confession shocked Dave. She *loved* having the upper hand sometimes.

"Don't play with me," he said. "You know what I'm talking about."

"Mr. Turner, I'm clueless. Maybe you can enlighten me," she purred as her fingers ran down the front of Dave's shirt.

She watched as Dave glanced around the parking lot before he brought his hypotonic eyes back to her. Her pulse sped up at the heated look in them. She was nervous about what he was going to do. This part of the parking lot was dark, but had enough light for them to see each other clearly.

"Are you sure you don't want to tell me again?" he asked as his index finger pulled the strap of her dress down her shoulder.

She tried not to shiver as the cool night air hit her exposed nipple. "I'm positive."

"Well, I guess I'll have to find a way to get it from you, won't I?" Dave asked as her second strap joined the first one. "Have I told you how beautiful your nipples are? They look like two perfect drops of chocolate. I could lick and suck at them all night."

"Hmmm... no you haven't." Charisma mumbled, trying not to break as Dave ran his palm over her left breast.

"Well. I guess it's time I give them their do respect." Dropping his head, he pulled only her nipple into his warm, wet mouth and sucked.

Charisma bit down on her lips to keep from screaming from the sheer pleasure of it. For some reason, the prospect of being caught made it even hotter. "Oh...that feels so good."

She felt Dave's smirk against her breast a second before he removed his mouth and latched on to the right breast. Thrusting a knee between her thighs, he shoved her legs as far apart as they would go. He gave her exposed nipple another long, hard suck before he let it go.

"Did that refresh your memory?" Dave inquired, brushing his knees over her soaked panties.

Grabbing his shirt, she yanked him to her and gave him a slow wet kiss that had both of them moaning before she finally let them up for air. "I think it may be coming back to me, but it's not quite there yet."

"I guess that means I need to find a way to get you to admit the truth," he sighed and spun her around, flattening her bare breasts against the cold car door. It shocked her body and excited the naughty side of her all at the same time.

"Spread you arms and place your hands flat against the door, ma'am. I heard that you took something from the restaurant. So, I'm going to have to search you," Dave whispered by her ear. "Are you still not remembering what happened back in the building? You know the truth will set you free."

"I'm sorry, sir, but I don't have a clue what you're talking about," Charisma answered, getting into the role play.

"Alright, that was your last chance. Now, it's time you get what you deserve. I'm going to search this sweet, tight body of yours and just maybe it will jog your memory."

Charisma chewed the inside of her jaw as Dave's hands started at her ankles and worked their way up until hit the hem of her dress. "I wonder what you're hiding under here," he exclaimed out loud as he slipped his hands underneath.

She almost died as Dave's stroked her wet folds with the tips of his fingers. "I think I found something already. I would have never guessed a classy lady like you didn't wear underwear. Were you hoping that a man might do this?"

Charisma clenched her teeth to keep quiet as Dave dipped his thumb inside of her. *This was so wrong*, she thought as she tried to keep her cool. Anyone could come from the restaurant and catch them like this. She had never been this free with another man in her life. Dave was brining out the bad girl in her.

"Please," she whimpered as Dave removed his thumb. She wanted more and he wasn't giving it to her.

"Please...what?" his warm breath whispered into her ear. "Are you saying that you want a further body search? You've been so bad all night. Maybe I do need to investigate a little more. You know that I am a private inspector."

"I've been bad...so I'm willingly to take the punishment I deserve," she confessed, wiggling her bottom against the front of Dave's slacks. The feel of his hard cock almost made her lose it right there.

"The punishment might be something hard and thick. Are you sure you're capable of handling it? I want to give you fair warning that the punishment can go on for hours. It usually doesn't stop until we are both completely satisfied."

Lord....why was he still talking when she wanted him to get on with it? She was beyond horny! The breezy night air wasn't cooling down her body in the least. Honesty, the feel of the cold truck on her swollen nipples was making her even hotter!

"I'm so ready..." she confessed. "Finish your body search."

"As you wish," came Dave's soft reply, but he pushed her short dress up back her waist baring her naked ass. Cupping her butt in one hand, he eased three thick fingers inside her tight core. "Come on, baby....tell me what I want to hear," he whispered as his digits worked in and out of her at a steady pace.

As the sounds of Dave's fingers working in and out of her body echoed around them, a tingling sensation started in the base of her spine. "Hmmm....that feels so good," she moaned, moving her hips to the same tempo.

"Good enough for you to tell me you love me again?" Dave asked then ran his tongue down the side of her neck.

"God....yes!" she screamed. "I love you. I love you so damn much," she screamed as she felt the first sign of an orgasm about to hit her and everything stopped.

"Finally," Dave groaned as he pulled down her skirt and stepped back. "The words I wanted." Spinning her around, he quickly fixed the front of her dress.

"What in the hell is wrong with you?" Charisma cried. Her body was wrung tight for the orgasm she didn't get. This was the second time he left her like this.

"Baby, don't be mad." Wrapping her up in his arms, Dave pulled her against his chest. "I want to take you back to our house and make love to you until neither one of us can get out of bed. This was a fun game and all, but I'm not going to make *love* to the woman I love in a dark restaurant parking lot."

All the anger evaporated from her body after hearing Dave's words, because she knew he meant what he told her. Now she truly knew how True and Jenisha felt when they fell in love with their husbands.

"You better live up to your promise," she answered, holding his eyes with hers.

Tenderly, his eyes melted into her. "Charisma, I would never tell you any lies. I love you too much for that. Let's go home so I can prove how much."

Chapter Twenty-Four

"Are you sure that I look okay?" Charisma asked for the fourth time as Dave drove down the highway back to his house. She wanted to make a good impression on his sister. He talked about Brittney so much that she knew his little sister meant a lot to him.

"Baby, you look very pretty," he replied, glancing over at her. "I know that Brittney will love you as much as I do."

She wasn't so sure about that. Dave might not realize that Brittney might think she was trying to take her older brother away. She had to make sure that she didn't come across as too cold or bitchy.

"I'm not going to celebrate until after I met her and see how it goes," Charisma answered. Butterflies appeared in her stomach as Dave drove into his driveway. She tried to calm down her nerves to take in the beauty of his house. It had to be the largest beach house she had ever seen. "Your house is amazing. I didn't think there were beach houses out here that big."

"Thanks. I've added some things to it over the years," Dave said, getting out of the car. Charisma waited while he came around and opened her door for her."

"You did a wonderful job," she praised as he closed the door and walked with him towards the front porch. She had to stand still and take it all in. The siding was light blue with white trim around the windows and doors. Gorgeous white wicker beach chairs were on the front porch, giving it a cozy and comfy feeling.

"If you're really good, later I'll show you the pool and private hot tub that I have out back. We can slip in there with a couple of drinks and enjoy ourselves. Or we can go down to the beach and enjoy the white sand," Dave whispered in her ear as he slipped his arms around her waist.

"Where is your sister going to be when we are doing all of this?" Lord, this man could make her lose her common sense so easily.

"I'll make sure she spends the night at a friend's house."

"No, I can't throw her out on the first night I get here. How about we all have dinner together, and I can get to know her better?"

"Do you really want to do that? Brit can be a handful for me, so I don't know how well you'll be able to handle her craziness," Dave asked, concerned.

"If I'm going to be in your life, I need to know your sister."

"There is no damn 'if 'about it. You're going to be in a life for a very long time, Charisma Miles," Dave promised, kissing the back of her neck.

"Oh, God. Do you have to do that outside so all my friends can see you?" a young female voice complained behind them.

Charisma tried to get out of Dave's arms, but he only tightened his hold and gave her another kiss before he moved away. Without a doubt, she knew Dave's sister was standing behind them, and she didn't sound very happy that Charisma was here.

"Don't worry, you'll do fine," Dave whispered before he spun her around to face Brittney.

The tall gorgeous blonde Charisma connected eyes with totally caught her off guard. She wasn't expecting someone so much different than Dave. "Hello. I'm Charisma Miles."

Titling her head to the side, Brittney studied her for a few minutes, then looked over at Dave. "Is this the woman you're in love with?"

"Yes, it is," he replied.

"Does she love you?"

"Yes, I do," Charisma cut in before Dave could answer.

A huge grin spread across Brittney's face. "Good. Because if you didn't, I would have told you to go back home. My brother doesn't deserve a woman who isn't totally into him. Oh, by the way, I'm pretty sure that you already know that I'm Brittney Turner, Dave's favorite little sister."

"You're my only sister," Dave exclaimed.

"I know and that's why you're going to give me forty bucks so I can go shopping with Rachel." Brittney snapped her fingers and held out her hand.

Charisma held back a laugh as Dave groaned before pulling out his wallet and handing his sister the money. "Here. Now don't spend it all in one place tonight."

"We're going shopping and then I'm going to spend the night at Rachel's. Her brother is home from college and he's a hottie."

"Rachel's brother is twenty and way too old for you."

"I didn't say I wanted to date him," Brittney complained and looked at him. "Anyway, your girlfriend is here, and I know that you probably want the place to yourself."

"Oh, I don't want you to leave because of me," Charisma said.

Brittney waved her comment off. "I'm always spending the night at Rachel's. She has the coolest room, and I want to pig out on pizza and chips. I can't do that with Dave. He's always eating all that healthy crap."

"All that junk food isn't good for you."

"Please don't give me another lecture. I'm on the track team at school. I eat healthy the rest of the week, so the weekends are mine. So, can I spend the night or what?"

Charisma hated the thought of Dave throwing his sister out because of her. She had wanted to spend some time with the young girl while she was here for the weekend. If Brittney was away until Monday, she wouldn't be able to do it.

"I want you back home by six o'clock Sunday night," Dave answered.

"Cool. I'll be home," Brittney grinned and ran past them into the house.

"Are you sure that she isn't leaving because of me?"

"No. Half the girls in the neighborhood have a crush on Rachel's brother. He looks like Colin Farrell, but he's a good kid. I know he won't do anything with Brittney."

"How can you be so sure? You're sister is very pretty."

"He doesn't want me to come over there and kick his ass."

"I get it now," Charisma laughed and planted her hand in the middle of Dave's chest. "How about you show me around the rest of your house?"

"I would love that a lot," Dave answered, then linked their hands together and led her towards his place.

Chapter Twenty-Five

The tepid breeze blew over her skin right before a pair of warm firm lips kissed her navel. "You're so damn beautiful. I want to spend the rest of my life with you. This has been the best three days of my life."

Charisma ran her fingers through Dave's thick black hair and relaxed more in the white lounger chair. She hadn't thought about work all the while she had been here and she loved it. But she would be leaving next week, and it hurt her to even think about going back home. "I've loved being here with you, too. You have made me feel so special."

"What about the rest?" he asked, lifting her out of the chair. He lay down and placed her on top of him. "Would you like to make a future with me?"

There would have been a time that she would have backed out of giving Dave an honest answer, but she wasn't living in that fear anymore. She was totally in love with all the muscles, tattoos, and the more-than-amazing man he was on the inside.

"Yes, I would marry you tomorrow if you asked me."

"That's what I wanted to hear." Picking her up, Dave sat her down and knelt down in front of her. Reaching into his pocket, he pulled out a small black box and held it under her nose. "Charisma Miles, I love you more than anything in the world, and I can't imagine you going back to California without a ring on your finger."

"Will you do me the wonderful honor of becoming my wife? I know that I'm not in the same league as the men you work with, but I'll give you all the money in the world to make up for the lack of money I have at the moment." Flipping open the box, he held it out to her and waited for her answer.

Tears slowly rolled their way down her cheeks. She couldn't believe this was happening to her. Was she really getting proposed to? Could she actually have the same things as Jenisha and True? Charisma swallowed hard and blinked back more tears.

"Are you sure?" she whispered.

"Am I sure about what?"

"That you want to marry me. I can be a little temperamental at times, and I would hate for you to regret proposing a couple of years into the marriage."

"Baby, I'm a hundred percent clear about what I am doing, and there isn't another woman for me in the world. You're the one, and I want you to be my wife. So will you marry me?"

"Yes, I'll marry you," Charisma screamed holding out her hand. "I love you too much not to become Mrs. Dave Turner." Holding out her hand, she let Dave slip on the ring and was surprise by how it was a perfect fit.

"YES!" Dave screamed. Picking her up, he swung her around and wrapped her up in his arms. "I'm never going to let you go."

"I hope not since you're the missing piece to my puzzle."

"You remember me telling you that?" Dave asked, staring into her eyes. "I was trying so hard to win you over back then."

"Yes, I remember, and that's when I knew I could fall in love with you. You were everything I was looking for in a man and husband, but I was scared to let go," she confessed.

"Well, I'm glad that you did, because the first time I saw you, I fell in love with you. I just hoped and prayed you didn't belong to someone else, because I would have stolen you from them."

"How do you know I would have gone?" Charisma questioned.

"I knew I had a chance from our first kiss at Jenisha's house when you didn't slap my face."

Circling her arms around Dave's neck, Charisma smiled at her future husband. "Do you know how bad you turned me on that day? I almost followed you out to your car and begged you to take me."

Dave squeezed her butt before he wrapped her legs around his waist. "I'm glad that you didn't, because I don't know if I had enough willpower then to push you away."

"But it didn't happen and look at where we are at now. We are going to get married. All we have to do is set a date."

"I have a date in mind," Dave whispered as he undid the back of her hot pink bikini."

"What? Two months from now?" she asked as the knot gave away.

"No, guess again."

"Six months?"

"Hell no!"

"Okay, I give up. When do you want us to get married?"

"In two days."

"WHAT?" Shoving Dave in the chest, Charisma got out of his embrace and fixed her top. "We can't get married in two days. It isn't possible. Things have to be done and Jenisha and True will kill me if they aren't at the wedding. No, we have to get married later on in the year."

Dave cupped her face in his hand and leaned down so she couldn't see anything but his gorgeous eyes. "Everything is already set up. I've been working on this since I came back from Jamaica. All we have to do is go and get the blood test. A friend of my works at the lab and he'll process the test today. We'll be good to go in two days. Don't you think a beach wedding will be beautiful?"

"You have been planning to marry me since Jamaica?" She couldn't believe this.

"Yes. I knew after the night I woke up without you in my arms that I didn't want it to happen again, so I took steps to make sure it wouldn't happen."

The idea of getting married in two days was starting to sound better, because it meant she could have another one with Jenisha and True later on. She wouldn't make True walk down the aisle while she was pregnant. "Can we have another wedding in California after True has her baby? I want her to stand up with me and Jenisha."

"I'm too much in love with you to say no. Besides, I'll get to celebrated being married to the most beautiful woman in the world twice. So it that a yes?" Soft kisses pulled at the corner of her mouth. Dave was trying to seduce her into saying yes, and it was working.

"Mr. Turner, you are so bad. How can I tell you no?" Charisma grinned.

"You can't, and that's because you love me," Dave said before he kissed her.

* * * *

"Charisma, you make a beautiful bride. Thanks so much for letting me stand up there with you. My brother is so happy," Brittney said, watching her while she watched her new husband talk to a waiter. Dave had gotten upset with the way the man's eyes lingered on her breasts. She needed to have a talk with him about that. He had to understand that now he was truly the only guy for her.

"Brittney, you're so welcome. I just glad you accepted my relationship with your brother and our quickie marriage."

"Oh, Dave is totally into you. A day never went by that he didn't mention your name."

She already knew how Dave felt, but it was so good to hear someone tell her about it. Dave was a good guy and he was all hers for the next fifty years. "Yeah, the feeling is mutual. I wouldn't know what I would do without him. I never met a man as honest or giving as Dave," Charisma said looking at her young sister-in-law.

Brittney eyes darted away from hers and over to Dave's like she was trying to hide a secret. She wondered what was going on. "Brittney, is there something wrong?"

"No," she replied a little too quickly. "I better go and get a piece of cake before it's all gone." Brittney quickly hurried away and got lost in the crowd on Dave's deck.

Charisma decided to let her worries about Brittney go. She remembered being a teenager and how her emotions were constantly up and down. She was missing her husband, and she was going to get him.

Going across the room, Charisma slipped her hands under Dave's jacket and placed them on his chest. "Can't you leave the poor guy alone now? He didn't mean any harm," she said. "Besides, I want to dance with my sexy new husband."

She waited while Dave gave the young waiter one last lecture before he turned around and kissed her. "I had to set him straight. No man is going to drool over my wife's perky breasts but me."

"You're so bad," Charisma giggled, but her heart warmed at the thought of Dave trying to protect her. "Are you going to have a talk with all the males on my roster, too? I see them looking at my breasts sometimes."

"Give me their names, and I'll do it," Dave growled and ruined it by smiling. "Do you know how much I love you?"

"Not more than I love you. However, I'm upset about something," she pouted.

"Tell me, and I'll fix it."

Stepping closer, Charisma rubbed her body against Dave's until she felt his cock hardened and lengthen. "I want to take my handsome husband upstairs and have my way with him, but I can't. There's a house full of people, so I guess it will have to wait until later."

Dave palmed her ass thrusting his erection against her stomach. "Why don't you go upstairs and get comfortable. I'll have all of these wedding guests gone in ten minutes or less?"

"Are you sure you don't need any help?"

Shaking his head, Dave moved back and walked her to the sliding doors. "No, I want you to have all of your energy saved for what I have in stored for you tonight. It is our honeymoon, after all."

"I thought it was wonderful that your parents volunteered to take Brittney back to the hotel with them," Charisma said.

"I know. It surprised me, too. So now we can eat naked in the kitchen for breakfast," Dave growled before he opened the door and gently shoved her inside. "Wear something sexy so I can strip it off you in a few minutes."

"I promise that you won't be disappointed, Mr. Turner."

Chapter Twenty-Six

Calloused hands explored the sleek line of her back before moving down to her waist and finally her hips. She moaned as teeth nibbled the middle of her back sending tiny electric shocks throughout her limbs. God, if she knew being married would feel this good, she would have dragged Dave to the altar months ago.

"Do you know what I want?" Dave asked, licking the sensitive area right at the side of her neck.

"I thought you got everything you wanted a few minutes ago," she purred, turning her neck to give Dave better access.

"I did, but I want something different now."

"What is it?"

"It's sticky and white."

"Like I said, didn't you already have that?" Charisma moaned. She flinched as Dave slapped her left butt cheek and sat her up in the bed. "You've a very dirty mind, Mrs. Turner. I wasn't talking about that."

"Then what do you want?" she said, rubbing her stinging cheek.

"Wedding cake. That icing was delicious, and I want to lick it off your body."

Pleasure lit up Charisma's eyes, and a huge smile covered her face. "Oh, let me go and get it. Maybe there is some of that champagne left to go with it."

"Are you sure? It's still our wedding night and I want to serve you, not the other way around." Dave started to roll out of the bed, but she pulled him back.

"No, let me. You're going to be working hard later anyway to get all of the sticky icing off me." Climbing out of bed, Charisma grabbed Dave's shirt off the floor and buttoned it up. "Don't you go anywhere. I'll be right back." She raced from the room as Dave leaned over the bed and made a grab for her.

Downstairs in the kitchen, Charisma was getting everything ready to take back to the bedroom when she noticed through the glass doors a wedding present outside on the patio. She thought that Dave had told her he already brought all of them in and placed them inside the extra bedroom.

Making her way over to the door, she unlocked it and grabbed the present and quickly shut the door. She looked down at the noted and noticed it was addressed to the happy couple from *Trish*.

Who in the world was Trish?

She didn't remember meeting her at the reception earlier. Curiosity was getting the best of her. She hadn't gotten to open any presents yet, because she couldn't wait to make love to her husband. Why couldn't she open this one? Dave wouldn't care. Going over to the kitchen table, she sat the box down and took off the white satin box. Lifting off the lid, she took out a photo album and was surprised to find another note attached.

I thought you might like to get to know the man you married a little better.

Opening the beautiful white album, Charisma turned to the first page smiling at the picture of Dave when he was about sixteen or seventeen years old. He wasn't a muscular as he was now, but anyone could see he was well on his way. She turned to the next page and saw Dave with his arm around a man's shoulder. The name Jackson was written on the bottom of the photograph.

"I know he has never mentioned anyone named Jackson to me before," she mumbled flipping to the next page. The next shot was Dave hugging a stunning redhead, and Charisma spotted the name Trish on her T-shirt.

Was she one of Dave's old girlfriends? No, it couldn't be because Dave told her he wasn't involved with anyone when they started dating. He wouldn't lie to her about something like that. Shaking off the weird feeling, she continued flipping through the album until an article made her stop.

Upcoming bodybuilder dies from steroid over dose. Jackson Kennedy was found dead in his hotel room from apparent body enhancers that were found scattered around his body.

Charisma shook her head. No, Dave wasn't a steroid user. Sure, he had a damn fine body, but he told her he worked out hard to get that away. He wasn't involved in any of this. She wanted to close the book, but something pushed her to continue. After seeing the next page, she wished that she hadn't. There was a picture of Dave wrapped up in Trish's arms kissing her. The reprinted date was the week after she had that huge fight with Dave in his truck. He lied to her! He had been cheating on her!

She told herself that she wasn't going to cry, but the tears started to fall anyway. What was wrong with her? Dave was the one who was wrong, and she was crying over that jackass. The hell she would. Getting up from the table, Charisma held the photo album against her chest and stormed back upstairs trying to ignore her breaking heart.

* * * *

"Were you going to tell me about this?" Charisma yelled at him before she tossed the photo album down on the bed next to him.

"What are you talking about? Where did you get this?" Dave asked, reaching for the album. He already knew what was in it without opening it up. Trish kept it by her bedside since Jackson died. Shit, how in the fuck did Charisma get a hold of it?

"It was a wedding present from your girlfriend Trish," she snapped as she took off his shirt and flung it on the bed.

"Trish isn't my girlfriend!"

Dave watched as Charisma hurried around the room and started to get dressed. He sat up in the bed in shock. Where in the hell did his wife think she was going at this time of night? "Sweetheart, what are you doing? It's late. Why don't you come back to bed, and we can talk about this in the morning?"

"I'm not doing anything with you, because I can't believe I fell for your line of crap. You were sleeping with Trish before you came to Jamaica and went back to her after we had our fight."

"I've never slept with Trish," Dave swore as he jumped out of the bed. "I wouldn't do that to you. I love you."

Charisma mumbled something under her breath as she slipped on her shoes and grabbed her purse off the night table by the closet. "Do you think I believe you? I had ex-boyfriend tell me the same lies. I won't take it from you."

She moved for the door, and he stepped in her path. He wasn't letting Charisma walk out on him on their wedding night. "First, I'm your husband. I'm not one of those losers you use to date in your past. I have never lied to you."

"Okay, I'll stay with you if you answer two questions. But if the answers are yes, you have to move and let me leave."

"Fine. I agree because the answers won't be yes," Dave replied confident.

"Have you ever shared a bed with Trish and did you ever go and break things off with her after we started dating?"

Dave felt his heart drop to the bottom of his stomach. Out of all the questions in the world, why did Charisma have to ask him those two? "Charisma, it isn't what you think. Trish…."

"Don't," Charisma interrupted, holding up her hand. "I just want to go home. I'll call you in a couple of days to let you know what I want to do." She brushed past him and was halfway out the door before he asked his question.

He hated to ask, but he did. "Do about what?"

"Our marriage," Charisma answered before she disappeared around the corner.

Chapter Twenty-Seven

A month later

"Are you ever going to call him back? He keeps calling Clinton to get information about you. He's so lonely without you. I wouldn't let a hottie like that go," True grinned, rubbing her stomach.

"I can't believe she got married without us," Keira mumbled.

"God, I can't believe she quit her job at the sports agency and is going to start her own with Ross as her first client. Our Charisma has a lot going on. Maybe we should give her a break," Jenisha said.

"Why can't all of you just leave me alone?" Charisma moaned, holding her throbbing head. She felt horrible, and it was all Dave's fault.

"Oh, don't worry. The morning sickness will pass sooner than you think," True said, sliding a plate of crackers over to her. "Just think. You're going to have a little Dave."

"Yeah, my husband's cheating on me while I'm pregnant. I'm over the moon with joy," Charisma grabbed a cracker, shoving it into her mouth. She fought back tears as she thought how happy he would be about the baby. He constantly told her how he wanted to start a family with her.

"I don't believe Dave is sleeping with that Trish chick. I think she was a jealous bitch and was trying to break the two of you up. No man looks at you the way he does while thinking about another woman," Jenisha pointed out.

"I have to agree with Jenisha," Keira said. "He isn't a jerk like that friend of his."

"Are you talking about Jim Russell?" Jenisha asked. "He has always been so nice to me."

"Well, he was rude to me. He told me to stay out of Dave's business. I hope I never run into that jerk again in my life."

"How about we get the conversation back on Charisma? I think she needs to call her husband and work this silly argument out. Dave is a good guy, and the two of you are the perfect couple." True picked up a cracker and took a bite.

"Do you think I overacted?" Charisma asked, looking at her friends. "I love Dave, and I honestly don't want to lose him. But all of that came as a shock."

"Well, if you want to know the whole story, I can tell you," Jenisha said. "Dave told us last night at our house."

Sitting up straighter in her chair, Charisma's heart started pounding in the middle of her chest. "Dave is in town?" She wanted to see her husband, but how could she face him after walking out on him on their wedding night.

"Yes, he is. He's staying at the hotel about a block from your house. He wanted to come see you the first night he got in, but he talked himself out of it."

"Jenisha, how long has he been here?" Charisma inquired.

"He got in the next night after you left. He has been nervous about coming to see you, so he left our house and checked into that hotel. Now, does that sound like a man who's in love with another woman? However, Clinton did mention to me this morning that Dave was leaving today because of a problem with Brittney."

Standing up, Charisma grabbed her purse off her chair. "I need to work things out with my husband. It was childish of me to run out like that, and I have to make things right." Waving good-bye to her girlfriends, she rushed for the restaurant.

* * * *

Arriving in Miami, Florida, Charisma quickly rented a car at the airport and headed for Dave's house. She went over her several apology speeches numerous times in her head, but she still didn't think any of them sounded right. How could she believe something from a total stranger and not her husband?

She had put Dave in the same category as her past boyfriends for so long that it took a while for her to see what a terrific man she had. Hopefully, he'll be willing to hear her out and not ask for a divorce. She was going to do everything in her power to save her marriage. Dave had every right to slam the door in her face without even listening to her.

"I pray that I haven't ruined the best thing that has ever happened to me," she mumbled, placing her hand over her stomach. Even if Dave threw her out on her ass, she was going to tell him about the baby. He deserved to be a part of his child's life. The rest of the drive to the beach house seemed to take forever, because she didn't know what the future held for her.

Turning the car into the driveway, Charisma sat there a few minutes and tried to get her thoughts together. This was going to work out for her. Taking a quick breath, she got out of the car and made her way toward the front door. Despite the fact she was married to Dave, she didn't feel right walking into his house unannounced.

"I'm just going to knock and let the cards fall where the may." Charisma knocked once and waited, but nothing happen. She raised her hand to knock again, but a sound behind her stopped. Pivoting, she found Brittney behind her staring a hole into her.

"Excuse me. What are you doing here? I thought you dumped my brother on your wedding night."

"Brittney, can you tell me where Dave is?"

"What do you want with him?"

"I need to talk to him. Can you please tell me where he is?

"Why should I?" Brittney snapped. "You were the one who broke my brother's heart."

Charisma hated to hear that Dave was in any kind of pain because of her. "I want to make up for that, but I can't without talking to him. I love Dave, and I was stupid for leaving him."

Brittney nodded at her. "You're right. You were stupid for mistreating my brother. He's such a nice person and you just walked all over him. I still don't think I should tell you where he is."

She could understand the girl's anger at her. "Fine, don't tell me. I'll just stay here until he comes home. I don't care if I have to sleep out here on the deck. I'm not going to leave until I see Dave."

"You really love my brother?"

"More than anything." *Please let her help me.*

"He's down on the beach. If you go down those steps," Brittney said pointing to the left, "you won't be able to miss him."

"Thank you," Charisma said and rushed to find her husband.

* * * *

Dave finished the last of his run and stopped to look out at the ocean. Today was one of the rare occasions that he had the beach to himself, but he wasn't happy at all. He missed the hell out of Charisma, and he was clueless at how to get her back. Why didn't he tell her about Jackson and Trish before that damn wedding present? He had so many chances and never took any of them. It was all his fault. He would give anything to hear Charisma say his name again.

"Dave?"

God, he really had it bad. He was hearing things now. Shaking his head, Dave tried clearing his mind. Charisma wasn't here, and she wasn't about to show up anytime soon.

"Dave!"

There it was again. The sound of Charisma's voice. It was almost like she was right behind him or something.

"Dave, why won't you turn around and answer me? Are you that mad at me?"

No, it couldn't be, he thought. Turning around slowly, Dave froze at the side of his wife behind him and was more scared than he cared to admit. He got his wish, but was it what he wanted?

The white sundress hugged every perfect curve of his wife's body. He wanted to sweep her up in his arms and carry her back in the house. It had been over six weeks since he had made love to her and he missed that closeness.

"What are you doing here?"

"I came to see you," Charisma said, moving closer until she was within touching distance. He shoved down the urge to run his fingers down the side of her face.

"Why did you come to see me?" he asked.

"I wanted to talk about our future."

Was he strong enough to let Charisma go? No, the hell he wasn't. He was a selfish bastard. He couldn't think about being a single man again. Not after enjoying the delights of being a married man.

"Do you want….a divorce?" Dave could barely get the words out of his mouth.

"No," Charisma shouted and took a quick breath. "I didn't come here for that. I came here to see if there was a way I could make you forgive me. What I did on our wedding night was so wrong. I reverted back to my old bitchy ways, and I wasn't proud of that Charisma."

Hope filled Dave as he slipped his arms around Charisma's waist and pulled her against his chest. "Don't blame yourself. I should have told you about Jackson and his addiction long before you found out. When I tried to stop him, it was too late. He wouldn't listen to me. Furthermore, I never slept with Trish after Jackson's death. I became her crutch, and she couldn't let me go."

"I could understand why she couldn't. You're hot as hell, and I could understand why she fell in love with you," Charisma said.

"It doesn't matter now. You're the only woman in my life. I don't want to start a family with anyone else but you, Mrs. Charisma Turner."

"That's good to hear since I'm six weeks pregnant," she grinned.

Dave moved back and placed his hand on Charisma's flat stomach. "Are you sure?" he whispered with pleasure in his voice.

"Two pregnancy tests and a trip to the doctor and all of them were a yes. I couldn't be happier. I thought I had everything I wanted until you came into my life."

"I guess you're pleased now that I took things into my hands that night at Jenisha's?"

"Yes, I am. I only have one regret," Charisma confessed.

"What is it?" Dave asked cupping her face in his hands.

"I didn't come to my senses sooner."

"That's okay. I have you now, and that's the only thing that matters," Dave breathed against her lips before he kissed her.

About the Author

Marie Rochelle is an award-winning author of erotic, interracial romance, including the Phaze titles *All the Fixin'*, *My Deepest Love: Zack*, and *Caught*. Visit her online at http://www.freewebs.com/irwriter/.

Lightning Source UK Ltd.
Milton Keynes UK
UKOW041827181212

203853UK00001B/8/P